Sigmund Bowman Alexander

A Moral Blot

A Novel

Sigmund Bowman Alexander

A Moral Blot
A Novel

ISBN/EAN: 9783337349127

Printed in Europe, USA, Canada, Australia, Japan

Cover: Foto ©Andreas Hilbeck / pixelio.de

More available books at **www.hansebooks.com**

A MORAL BLOT

A NOVEL

BY

SIGMUND B. ALEXANDER

AUTHOR OF "WHO LIES?" "THE VEILED BEYOND," "JUDITH,"
"TEN OF US," ETC.

What mockery is at the root of laws that rust
In creeds of pre-election so unjust
If sin be sin, what preference bids it scan
With lowering looks of punishment and ban
The woman it enslaves and soils, yet pause to absolve the man.

EDGAR FAWCETT

BOSTON
ARENA PUBLISHING COMPANY
COPLEY SQUARE
1894

AFFECTIONATELY DEDICATED

TO

FLORRIE, GRACE, ALFRED, LOUIS

AND STANLEY.

CONTENTS

PART I.

THE THORN UPON THE ROSE.

PART II.

THE SPOT UPON THE TIGER LILY.

PART I.

THE THORN UPON THE ROSE.

Ver. " I pluck this pale and maiden blossom here
　　　Giving my verdict on the white rose side."
Som. " Prick not your finger as you pluck it off."

SHAKSPERE (Henry VI).

A MORAL BLOT.

CHAPTER I.

THE SCRIBE.

"As we are poetical in our natures, so we delight in fable."
HAZLITT.

"Fables take off from the severity of instruction and enforce it at the same time that they conceal it."
ADDISON.

. . . "Much talk about him that I should like to know your Scribe."

Two gentlemen were walking along Tremont Street amid a throng of theatre-goers, leaving the Boston Museum after an evening performance, and the elder was speaking. "Come," he continued, "let's go to Billy Park's for a little lunch."

"Do you really mean, then, to say that the identity of 'The Scribe' is a mystery to you?" queried the younger, as they turned down a side street. "It's an open secret."

"Do you know it?"

"Of course, and so does every one in Bohemia."

"But I am not one of the favored mortals from that abode of the blessed."

"He makes no secret of his identity, although he writes under a *nom de plume*, and if you care to meet him I will gladly introduce you. He's my particular friend and a good fellow, worth knowing."

"I imagined as much, from his writings," said Durrell, "and your statement as to his friendliness with you only serves to confirm the idea. By-the-way, have you seen this week's paper?"

"No, but I suppose he has a parable in it, as usual," replied Less. "We can see it in

here," he continued, as they entered the res-
taurant.

" And waiter," said Durrell when they had
laid aside their coats and ordered lunch,
"bring us a copy of this week's *Hermes.*
Yes, here it is," he cried, glancing through
the paper which the waiter handed him.
" A short one."

" Read it," said Less.

" All right," and in a subdued tone Durrell
read the following to his companion :

" And in the course of their travels Hassan
and Ahmed climbed a great mountain. As they
neared the summit they espied an inn, and being
aweary, said, ' Lo, here will we tarry for a time.'
And Ahmed sat himself down upon a bench before the door to gaze about at his leisure, the
while Hassan entered the house and ordered their
meal. And being a-hungered, Hassan did eat at
once of the fare set before him, pausing only to
call to his companion, ' Come Ahmed, to the
board and partake of the fare our host hath provided. By Allah, it is good ! '

" And this was blasphemy.

" And Ahmed sat without gazing down into the valley where Nature, wondrously beautiful, lay unveiled before him. Green plains and woods, dotted with white houses and villages, and in the distance the great city with its spires and minarets from which the soft breath of the breeze bore to his ears the faint music of bells. And the rivers and brooks winding like blue and silver ribbons over the verdant carpet that covered the nakedness of the earth. And the rugged, towering, snow-capped mountains reflecting the light of the sunbeams, and above all the wondrous blue of the heavens, over which now a fleecy cloud, now a soaring bird, floated gracefully. And the beauty of it all entered the soul of Ahmed and filled him with joy and wonder, so that he heard not Hassan and forgot his hunger and weariness in the sight; and while thus rapt in contemplation of Nature's loveliness he murmured, ' Allah, how beautiful ! '

" And this was prayer."

" Good ! " exclaimed Ingraham, as Durrell finished reading.

" Yes, sir, it is clever," said Durrell emphatically, "I must know that chap. Who is he, anyway?"

"Talk of the—angels," said Less, as he glanced towards the door. "Let him speak for himself."

A good-looking young man of medium height entered as he spoke, and with a smile of recognition approached their table in answer to a beckoning hand. "Hullo, Less," he exclaimed cordially, "What are you doing here."

"Same as you, I presume. Are you alone?"

"Yes, just came from the Museum."

"Well, sit down here with us. Let me present Mr. Charles Durrell, manager of the Folly Dramatic Company, Mr. Leo Ormsby; 'The Scribe.'"

"Very pleased to meet you, Mr. Ormsby," said Durrell heartily, "we were just discussing your last parable in *Hermes*."

"Yes?"

"Didn't see you in the theatre, Leo," observed Less.

"Were you there? How did you like the play?"

"Oh, so, so."

"What did you think of it, Mr. Ormsby?"

"Very little."

"It is quite a clever play."

"From a financial standpoint, perhaps. There are signs in it that the author is capable of doing good work, but I suppose if he did his best managers would reject the work, as publishers have rejected manuscripts of mine, saying, That is too good to make any money out of."

"There's a great deal of truth in that," assented Durrell.

"This age is a poor one for authors and artists, it is too matter-of-fact," said Leo. "To reach the highest place their art offers—and surely without the ambition to do so they can never hope to do anything worth

doing—they must spend their lives a-dream-
ing, in giving the imagination full play and
vitalizing the conceptions which dreaming
gives birth to. When they have to join in
the common scramble for bread and butter,
like ordinary mortals ; to give up their ca-
prices through sheer necessity ; they become
tainted, as it were, and the standard of
their productions is lowered until they are
no longer works of art. The 'pot-boiler'
quenches the fires of genius and poisons
ambition."

"Surely you can write as you please ? "

" Oh, yes, I was not speaking of any per-
sonal experience, but from general observa-
tion. I have been particularly fortunate.
The editor of *Hermes* expects a little from
me every week, and what I do for him is the
extent of my literary work, thus far. I am
an artist by profession, you know ; Less and I
have adjoining studios in Bohemia."

" While you are talking shop, Leo," said

Less, "tell me, have you found a model for your Diana, yet?"

"No, not yet. Do you know some one?"

"No, but perhaps Charlie can help you out. There are some 'hummers' in his company."

"I will be glad to introduce Mr. Ormsby to the hummers," said Durrell, smilingly.

"You just notice 'Tiger Lily' Leo, that's all," said Less, with a significant wag of his head.

"Who is Tiger Lily?"

"My leading lady," answered Durrell, "on the programme she is called Miss Laurence Varney."

"You can find material for a parable there," volunteered Less.

"How so?"

"Oh, work in some of your moral reflections on high kicking."

Durrell laughed.

"That subject is hardly in my line."

"Oh, come, Leo," cried Less, "don't pose as a purist."

"I have no such intention. I don't pretend to be a whit better than the next man. I am human, and therefore not above temptation."

"As for me," said Less, gayly, "speaking in the vein of your parables, if temptation seeks me not, then do I hie me forth to seek temptation."

"Do you know what you need, Less?" asked Leo seriously.

"Lots of things; money principally."

"I might put the question differently, and I am in earnest, old man. Do you know what would do you the most good?"

"Give it up; a quart of Pommery, perhaps."

"To marry some nice girl," said Leo.

"What! me?" exclaimed Less in unfeigned astonishment.

"Why not? Is there anything very dreadful in the idea? It would make an end of your knocking about, settle you down, in fact, and that's what you need."

"Maybe you're right, Leo," said Less, "but I haven't run across the right girl yet, and when I do she will probably not be an heiress, so I shall not be able to marry her."

"I did not think you were mercenary, · Less."

"Nor am I, no amount of money could induce me to marry a girl I did not care for, but my tastes are so refined and my pocket so slender that if I indulge in the luxury of a wife she must be one who is able to take her part in the realization of my ideas of refinement. A wife is expensive, so is refinement, and I can't support both alone."

"There's love in a cottage—" began Durrell.

"With bacon and greens, eh?" interrupted Less. "Excuse me, I prefer canvas-back duck."

"You ask too much, Less," said Leo.

"I know it, and I'm not likely to get it. If I do, well and good ; if not, I'm quite comfortable as I am, thank you. As for bacon and greens—bah ! "

"I'm sorry to hear you talk so, Less," returned Leo, "because as long as you entertain such ideas you will never be a great artist."

"How does that follow ? " asked Durrell, curiously.

"Naturally enough, according to the theories of one of my college professors."

"What are these theories ? I cannot conceive what connection a man's views upon matrimony can have with his achievements as an artist."

"I will try to explain. An artist's aim is to conceive and produce for his fellow-men that which is beautiful. Beauty is always the nearest expression or suggestion attainable of the *best*. Best is a vague term, however, varying with our conceptions. Nature never gives us a perfect object ; every advance to the best opens the way to a higher best. Outward forms seem beautiful to us because they are indicative of functional, or inward perfection, as, for instance, health in man. It is impossible to dissociate perfect physical from moral beauty, for in order to attain that health which gives physical beauty we must exercise certain moral qualities. Physical nature can be improved by moral nature."

"That's all very pretty and very true, but what has it to do with the question in hand ?" asked Less.

"A great deal, for it leads up to the fact that the man who leads an intemperate life cannot produce a work of art, since his hand and eye must have moral training. The finest work is not accomplished by intellectual power alone, moral power is required —the power of conceiving ideal beauty and idealizing every one of our actions, and, most of all, our own characters and lives."

" Well ?"

" Well, such sentiments as you express must, so long as you harbor them, affect your character, and your character must have a direct influence upon your work."

" Such fine æsthetic deductions are altogether too much for me."

"Æsthetic they are, I admit, and perhaps they may appear extreme ; if so, think them over, there is more in them than may appear at first, but I don't mean to preach a sermon, let us change the subject."

" I'm agreeable," said Less, good-naturedly, "the discussion of the prospects for reforming your obedient has little interest for me. I know him to be a hopeless case, past reform."

"But a royal good fellow, Less, whom I hope to retain as a friend," said Leo, smilingly.

" Just as long as you'll have me, old man," cried Less heartily.

" Did you ever try writing for the stage, Mr. Ormsby ?" inquired Durrell.

"I have two or three manuscripts lying in my studio somewhere that have been submitted to managers and returned with thanks, unread, I suspect."

" Did you sign them, 'The Scribe' ?"

" No, I used my own name."

" That was a mistake."

"Perhaps so."

"I may be able to assist you in finding a market for your plays ; I can get them read for you at any rate."

" Thank you, I may take advantage of your kind offer."

" Do so.   What are your works, dramas ?"

" No, no, nothing so ambitious. Principally little comediettas."

" Ah, curtain raisers."

" Yes."

"Have you nothing more pretentious ?"

" Yes, one piece ; I don't know just what to call it. It is founded on Longfellow's 'King Robert of Sicily,' but does not follow the story over closely. It is not exactly a burlesque, but it comes near being one."

"A burlesque !" exclaimed Durrell, "that's right in my line, and I want a new piece, too. You must let me see it."

"I will do so with pleasure, but it is not a burlesque in the accepted sense of the word."

"Never mind what it is, if it suits my people, and I decide to do it, they will make a burlesque of it soon enough."

"Well, I will send you the manuscript if you wish me to."

"Good. I am at Clark's," said Durrell.

"And now I must be going," said Leo, rising as he spoke. "I hope we shall meet again, Mr. Durrell."

"We shall, am I not to see your play ?"

"True. Good-night."

"Good-night."

And Leo left the pair in the now almost deserted cafe, smoking their fragrant havanas over the remains of a dainty lunch.

He had absorbed some of the romance from the play he had witnessed, just enough to color his thoughts, and the still, calm, starry beauty of the November night strengthened the sentimental mood he was in. He walked slowly and meditatively, letting his thoughts wander idly, but amid the play of fancy in his mind there was ever present the vision of a fair face, full of the freshness of youth, embowered in a halo of golden hair, from which the deep blue eyes sparkled and the cherry lip pouted and smiled with charming witchery.

"My Rose," thought the young man ecstatically, "my sweet, my fragrant Rose, she is—what? A woman only. That is all she can be, all I can desire. I must not be

like those who, when they feel that they love,
picture the object of their affections as an
ideal, which, if she is human, she is bound to
fall below. Every one has vulgar traits, and
every lover tries not to see these traits in
his mistress, tries so hard that he blinds
himself for a time, by raising her into the
realms of idealism ; but the higher he raises
her the greater will be her fall, for the fall
must inevitably come when his sight is restored. It is after this awakening to cold
reality that real love begins ; when a couple
thoroughly realize that they are but man
and woman, poor clay, after all, without a
particle of fanciful romance in them, outside
of their imaginations. Then true, deep, ay,
and real romantic, love begins—a love with a
substantial foundation, a love to last forever.
A love like mine for Rose. Yes, although
I have not reached that stage of familiar-
ity that forces a man to realize that his
idol is but clay, yet I am a dreamer, an habit-

2

nal dreamer, and so am able to realize the shallowness of dreams. My love is no dream, it is reality itself, and I must tell Rose of it very soon : not that the little puss does not know I am her slave as well as I do myself, but it is best that I should tell her in so many words. This friendship, this constant companionship we have lived in is very nice, but I feel it is time to bring about an actual understanding, even though Rose and I are sure of each other. A tacit understanding is all very well, but I want something more tangible. Ah, what a sweet little wife she will make, bless her ! "

Thus meditating, he crossed the Common and entered the new streets on the Back Bay. He paused before a cosy, but unpretentious little dwelling, and drew forth his keys. As he did so the door opened, and a gentleman descended the steps, after bidding some one "Good-night."

" Doctor Farnsworth," exclaimed Leo, as

he caught sight of the gentleman's face in the gleam of a street-lamp. "Is any one ill?"

"Ah, Mr. Ormsby, is it you?" said the doctor, cordially. "Yes, Mrs. Maynard has had another of her attacks to-night."

"It is nothing serious I hope?"

"Well," replied the doctor, dubiously, "she is all right for the present."

"You do not mean——"

"As you are a member of the household I will tell you; but remember, Miss Rose does not know how serious the matter is. She is not even to be told of my visit to-night."

"I understand."

"No one but Mr. Choate has been told what I am about to confide to you. Mrs. Maynard's trouble is from her heart; her attacks are increasing in violence and frequency; I can do nothing for her, and if they continue, as I fear they will, they are liable to carry her off very suddenly. Any shock or excitement may bring them on, still I do not wish you to think there is no hope. She may live many years yet, but it will always be with this menace hanging over her. In case of emergency it is well that some of the household should know, and Mrs. Maynard insists that Miss Rose be kept in ignorance."

"Yes, that is as well, Rose would only worry herself ill."

"Let us hope, however, that my fears are groundless," continued the doctor.

"Let us hope so."

"And now, good-night."

"Good-night."

The two men separated ; the doctor walking smartly away while Leo entered the house, careful to make no sound that might disturb the sick woman. He was met in the hall by a hale-looking elderly gentleman to whom he nodded and whispered, "How is she, Mr. Choate ?"

"Sleeping."

"Poor Rose," thought Leo.

"You are late, to-night," observed Choate.

"Yes, I met Less and a friend of his after the play."

"I don't like to seem an old fogy, Leo," said Choate, "but I want to presume on our old friendship so far as to offer you advice. Drop Lester Ingraham's company. He is a notoriously fast young man, and his society cannot benefit you. A man is known by the company he keeps, and a rising young fellow like you should be cautious."

"Pshaw!" replied Leo, "you speak so because you don't know Less. I have known him for years; we went to school together, and I think I understand him thoroughly. A more honest, whole-hearted fellow, I defy you to find. There is nothing false in him, and as for his life, why the very fact that his escapades are so generally known goes to prove that there is no duplicity about him; that he does not try to hide his doings by assuming a hypocritical virtue before people at whom he is slyly laughing in his sleeve, as some fellows I can point out do. Mind you, I don't approve of his life, but because we are friends is no reason that I should follow in his footsteps. Perhaps I may be the means of reforming him. Who knows ?"

"That may all be," said Choate, shaking his head dubiously ; "still——"

Leo ran upstairs with a hurried "good-night," as if to escape a lecture. Choate gazed after him with an odd look.

"A formidable rival," he muttered.

CHAPTER II.

THE ROSE.

" A rosebud set with little wilful thorns."
TENNYSON.

MRS. MAYNARD was the widow of a colonel
of the United States Army, and supported
herself and her daughter principally upon the
meagre pension which his grateful country
had awarded her after her husband fell,
fighting the Indians. To add to her limited
income she took her husband's old friend,
Oliver Choate, and Leo Ormsby, the play-
fellow of her daughter's childhood, into her
household ; knowing them both well, and
having plenty of room. The gentlemen appreciated the home they thus secured, and
lived contentedly under her hospitable roof.

Leo Ormsby was, as has been intimated, an artist with literary tastes and, unlike the majority of his brethren of the palette and pen, was able to make his talents yield him a competence. His parents died when he was quite young and left him to the care of a maiden aunt who, after giving him a good education, died also, leaving him, at the age of twenty, alone in the world but in comfortable circumstances. It was after the death of this good lady that he became a member of the Maynard household.

Oliver Choate had been the life-long friend of Colonel Maynard and, although a bachelor himself, found great pleasure in his friend's married happiness ; and as the years passed, he watched, with ever-increasing sympathy and interest, the growth and development of the little Rose. On the death of his friend he preferred making his home with the widow to keeping up his bachelor establishment, and many wondered at his choice ; for he was known to be a very wealthy man, and the magnificence of his bachelor quarters was proverbial among his acquaintances, while at Mrs. Maynard's he found no such luxurious appointments ; still it was homelike, and he was content since he had the companionship of his friend's widow and her child, the little Rose, whose blossoming from childhood to girlhood, and girlhood to womanhood, he had watched with eager interest—an interest that increased daily, although, for a time, he was unconscious of it, and when, at length, knowledge dawned upon him, it was bitter. Sometimes, sitting in the room where Rose was, he would pretend to read, but all the while his eyes would be fixed upon the girl, with a look of desire that seemed out of harmony with his gray hair. He had lived a lonely, loveless life, and now in his declining years, as if in mockery, Cupid had pierced his leathery old heart, and the sting of the shaft was as sharp as if he were a younger

man.   IIe felt the folly of his position, but so
keen, so all devouring was his passion that
he was unable to tear himself from the home
of Mrs. Maynard, and so he lingered on,
beneath the same roof that sheltered the object of his affections, eating his heart out
with a hopeless and almost unholy love and
hoping without hope.

Mrs. Maynard was a quiet, motherly
woman, with but one thought, one idea—
Rose ; blind to her every fault and too conscious of her good qualities ; Rose, the de-
murest little woman in Boston, full of art-
ful mischief, ever ready for some prank, but
serious, too, when she chose to be ; impul-
sive, fond of reading—especially the parables in *Hermes*—able to say a sharp thing
when her temper was roused, and somewhat
unforgiving, headstrong, and inclined to
forming biased opinions, discontented because of the many economies their circumstances forced her and her mother to practise,

jealous of her more fortunate girl-friends,
but politic enough to conceal her feelings
and assume an air of content, which was but
a screen hiding the constantly-increasing
bitterness in her heart, and—perhaps because she was an only child, petted and
spoiled—very selfish.

On the day following her illness Mrs.
Maynard appeared as well as ever ; perhaps
she assumed an ease she did not feel to
deceive Rose, and if so, she was perfectly
successful.

During the next few days Leo had several
interviews with Durrell in regard to his play
" King Robert of Sicily " : which had made
a good impression upon the manager; and
after some little discussion it was arranged
that Leo should re-write the play, in certain
parts, and if the alterations proved satisfac-
tory, Durrell was to produce it. In order
that the work should be made to fit the re-
quirements of his company, Durrell insisted

that Leo should come with him to New York, where the company was playing, to see them act, to meet them all', and to get their ideas.

" It is essential to your success," said Durrell, " and we don't play in Boston this season. To be sure, we do a number of one-night stands around here, and the company may be in town for a day or so, but that will give you no time, so you must come to New York."

So it was settled that Leo should go, and when Lester Ingraham heard of the arrangement he suddenly discovered that he, too, had urgent business in the metropolis and declared his intention of accompanying them. They laughed when he told them, but were glad of his company, for Less was an agreeable fellow, with no ambition greater than a desire to amuse himself and his friends, and an income that permitted him to realize his aim. He was a very taking man,

reputed fast—in fact, one of the useless orna-
ments of society; but his friendship was
no hollow sham, and beneath the aimless-
ness and lazy good-nature which characterized
him, lurked a quality which attracted Leo
and firmly cemented their friendship, a
rare quality—sincerity.

Leo worked hard at his writing during the
few days previous to his departure. He had
not only to put his play into shape, but also
to leave with the editor of *Hermes* enough
matter to fill his department of the paper
during his absence. Every moment he could
spare was spent with Rose, every thought
aside from his work was of her, and she
knew it. Although no words of love or marriage had been spoken by the young people,
each felt that words would be but the hollow
formality betrothing them before the world ;
that whether the words were spoken or not
they were none the less tacitly plighted, and
Choate, living in the same house with them,

could not but see and understand the state of affairs.

He felt a helpless despair and a growing bitterness towards his youthful rival that showed itself in innuendoes, principally regarding Leo's friendship for Less, insinuating that they were birds of a feather, and causing a vague unrest in Mrs. Maynard's motherly heart. But the young people were oblivious of it all.

Several days before Leo left for New York Choate was summoned to the great city on important business. It was with the utmost reluctance that he thought of leaving a clear field for Leo, but there was no alternative. His worriment began to tell upon him, and Rose, noticing his altered appearance, asked :—

"Are you ill, Mr. Choate ?"

"I believe I am," he replied.

"What is the trouble ?"

· "I—I can't tell," he stammered jokingly,

in deadly earnest, "I think I must be in love."

Rose laughed heartily. "Oh, Mr. Choate, who is she? The idea of your being in love!"

"Is the idea so preposterous?" he asked earnestly. "Do you not believe I could make a woman happy? Why, consider my wealth, —I could gratify every whim of my wife; think, would not hers be an enviable position?" He spoke tremulously, but with an intensity that was unusual, and which caused her to regard him curiously.

"Could this old man be in love with her?" she thought. "He had certainly been acting strangely of late, hinting at——He was wealthy; every one knew that: and if——" She was lost in a brown study for a moment.

"You do not answer me," said Choate.

"Most certainly the picture you paint is a tempting one, Mr. Choate; but you are joking."

" But if I were not joking—if, for example, you were the one to whom I proposed offering my all, what would you say then ? "

" I should say—well, I should want time to consider what I should say," she answered, as she tripped smilingly away.

Choate watched her departing form with glittering eyes, and muttered, as he moistened his parched lips, "Perhaps, perhaps yet——"

In the evening, as was their custom, Choate, Mrs. Maynard and Rose were gathered about the lamp in the sitting-room. In an hour Choate was to leave, and his mind was filled with unquiet thoughts. By gradual stages he led the conversation to the topic uppermost in his mind.

" And, all things considered, Mrs. Maynard," he said, pursuing the subject, "you honestly believe in love-marriages ? "

"I do, most decidedly," replied the lady.

" Let me put a case, suppose Rose had two

suitors, let us say, for example, Leo and—and myself——"

"Oh, Oliver !"

"As an example selected at random let it be as I say. Well, Leo's means are limited, mine unlimited,—would you prefer giving your child to Leo with an uncertainty for a future, or to me with a well-founded surety ?"

"Certainly you could offer her greater comforts, but——"

"Now, Miss Rose," interrupted Choate, "what would your decision be in such a case ?"

"Carefully, Rose !" cried Leo gayly as he entered the room. "I have heard enough to know that you are about to choose between Mr. Choate and me. Should he win your favor I will no longer respect his gray hair, let him bewar-r-r-r-r-e !"

"Now, now, Leo, quit fooling," cried Choate irritably, "and let Rose answer seriously."

3

"All right, fire away, Rose, and don't be
hard on poor Mr. Choate, you know he leaves
us to-night."

"As for me," said Rose, "I love creature-
comforts, and that would make me lean
towards wealth——"

"Ah!" from Choate.

"But if I repented."

"What then?"

"I might lead Crœsus an awful dance. As
it is, here is a hand for each; one for you,
Mr. Choate, and one for Leo, so both should
be satisfied."

"I have the hand nearest the heart!"
cried Leo.

"But I have the right one!" muttered
Choate.

"How strangely Mr. Choate talked," said
Mrs. Maynard to Rose, when they were alone.

"He spoke as if he meant what he said."

"Nonsense, child."

"No, Mummy, honest ; and suppose he did ? "

"Well, suppose he did ? "

" Well, would it be so awful ? "

" Why, Rose ! "

"I don't think it would. I tell you, mother dear, the way we have had to pinch since poor papa died has taught me a lesson and—and all in all, I do not think it would be so very dreadful."

" My dear," said Mrs. Maynard, gravely, "the heart is a tyrant that can make itself cruelly felt when all else is at rest ; never try to deceive yourself into believing that you can silence its cravings ; for you cannot do it."

" What a sentimental old Mummy you are, to be sure. I—I have no heart, I believe."

Mrs. Maynard laughed.

On the evening before Leo's departure

Mrs. Maynard felt it her duty to call upon her next-door neighbor, perhaps because the sympathetic lady wished to give Leo a chance to say a last sad farewell; there was no sadness about the interview, however.

"Is your parable written yet, Leo?"

"No, I must write it to-night before retiring."

"My! that will keep you up so late, and you know late hours are so injurious to little boys. Go right up to your room now and write."

"I would, Rose, only you are alone."

"Don't mind me. I am able to take care of myself, and I can read the dictionary or some such book which will entertain me quite as well as you can."

"My dear girl," cried Leo, "you entirely misunderstand me: if it were only a question of keeping you company or entertaining you I would go at once; but the fact is I feel as if I wanted a little company myself, and as you see, I kill two birds with one stone. I did think of calling upon Miss Russell, but she lives at some distance, and then there is the trouble of dressing, so I thought I might as well put up with what was at hand."

"Well, I never! I'll just leave you alone," cried Rose, rising in mock anger.

"Then I'll write my parable," returned Leo coolly.

"No, you won't," exclaimed Rose decisively as she reseated herself upon the *tete-a-tete* at his side, " I'm going to stay here and talk to you until midnight, so that you will have to work away into the morning to finish your writing and you won't get a wink of sleep."

"Oh dear !" said Leo, "how very dreadful, I thought you said a moment ago that you did not approve of late work for me."

"I've changed my mind since."

" Indeed ?   I thought I missed some little thing about you.   What did you change it for ? "

Now, Leo, I think if you—" she paused abruptly.

" Well ? "

" Oh, never mind."

" But I do mind."

" I'm sure you don't mind me."

" My dear child," said Leo with a pedantic air,"pray don't abuse our language ; when you wish to say obey don't say mind."

" Pshaw ! "

" Don't know him."

" Who ? "

" Shaw."

"Oh, Leo, seriously, I had a letter from Mary Shaw to-day and she sent some word or other to you," said Rose, diving her hand into the folds of her skirt in search of that mystery, a woman's pocket, from which, having at length located it, she drew a letter.

"Here it is. She says—let me see—oh, yes, 'tell Leo that Emily and I—': I guess I won't read it to you."

"Let me read it then."

"No, siree."

"But the message is for me."

"I decline the office of messenger."

"I'm dying of curiosity, Rose; do let me see it," and he extended his hand towards the letter.

With a merry laugh she put her hands behind her, and, looking saucily up at him said, "Get it if you can."

"You won't give it to me?"

"No, sir."

"And you defy me to take it from you?"

"Yes."

"I cannot employ force, as you are of the feminine gender, gallantry forbids. How am I to get it?"

"Use strategy."

"Well, then, first to bring your hands from behind you."

"If you do that you shall have the letter."

"Very well, but as I may not use force you must agree not to get angry at any of my manœuvres."

"I do."

"Now for it. In order to get that letter I shall have to suffer my face to be slapped," he murmured thoughtfully.

"What do you mean?"

"First move of the campaign," he exclaimed, and bending over, kissed her full on the lips.

"Oh Leo!" cried Rose, drawing away blushingly.

"You are at liberty to slap my face for it," he said calmly.

"Yes, and bring my hands forward to do it, and then lose my letter. No, sir."

"Second move of the campaign," he said, kissing her again.

" Leo Ormsby, if you do that again you'll be sorry for it."

" Do you surrender ? "

" No."

" Third move of the campaign."

As Leo bent over to kiss her for the third time Rose suddenly moved her head forward, so that, instead of their lips meeting in a kiss, their heads came together with an ignoble bump.

"Oh ! " exclaimed Rose, and startled by the force of the shock she lifted her hand to her head.

"Caught ! " laughed Leo, "the letter is mine."

" Yes, there it is," and she tossed it to him ; "but I think you're real mean."

" *I* didn't bump your head."

" No, but you—" Rose checked herself and blushed.

"I know it," cried Leo, laughingly, "and I glory in the act."

"It is hard to think of you as acting at all," returned Rose. "You spend so much of your time a dreaming."

"I admit your charge," he replied promptly, "but when in such charming company as I now am, my dreams are banished by the greater attractions of the loveliness before me."

"Taffy!" ejaculated Rose, with a blush.

"But," continued Leo, smilingly, unmindful of her interruption, "although you drive my dreams away when you are present, yet when you are absent the thought of you is the most potent charm I know of to set me castle-building again. Strange, what a paradox you are."

"Perhaps you are the paradox," she answered saucily.

"Perhaps I am," he said gravely. "Say, Rose, what shall I bring you from New York, as a peace-offering?"

"I don't know," she replied uneasily.

"I do."

"Do you?"

"Yes, dear, a ring, a diamond ring, the symbol of our——"

"Well, how have you been getting along in my absence?" cried Mrs. Maynard, as she entered the room.

Rose heaved a sigh of relief.

"I'll tell you about it later, dear," whispered Leo, and Rose gently pressed his hand as she left his side to help her mother with her wraps. But Leo found no opportunity to speak again, Rose took good care of that.

The next day he bade them good-bye, and as he lingered for a moment beside Rose he whispered, "I shall bring the ring with me, darling." In the next number of *Hermes* Rose read a parable that she felt sure she had inspired.

THE PARABLE.

There once lived a wondrously beautiful maiden, whose hand was sought in marriage by a certain rich and a certain poor youth. And it happened that both suitors were fearful of declaring their love to the maid.

Meeting, one day, they agreed to refer the matter to the high priest. And the high priest spake unto them, saying, "Thus shall it be decided. Ye shall both make offering to the Gods at the twelfth hour, and he whose offering is most pleasing, to him shall the maid be given, and he shall take her to him for his wife." And at these words the rich man laughed and rejoiced exceedingly and the poor man was cast down.

And the rich man hied him home and at the twelfth hour came unto the temple attended by a great train, and laid many rich and costly gifts upon the altar. And he looked about him for the poor man, to see what his offering might be, but saw him not, whereupon he smiled in great content and returned home, and caused himself to be arrayed in rich robes to await the coming of his bride.

And the poor man went sorrowfully from the high priest's presence, for he knew he could make the Gods no fit offering, yet was he conscious of a purity of heart. And so he wandered amid fields and groves, and the beauty of nature soothed his troubled spirit, and when the twelfth hour was come, he cried, " The Gods are good, for they give me these beauties to live amidst, and if they deny me my heart's desire surely it is because they deem it for the best." And, lo! as he spake he saw the maiden approaching, and she smiled on him and he took her in his arms, his heart filled with a great, holy joy, and she was his.

CHAPTER III.

THE TIGER LILY.

" When lovely woman stoops to folly,
And finds too late that men betray,
What charm can soothe her melancholy,
What art can wash her guilt away ? "

OLIVER GOLDSMITH.

" GOOD-MORNING, Mr. Ingraham," said
Oliver Choate as he met Less in the cor-
ridor of the Imperial Hotel, " is Leo in New
York yet ? "

" Not yet, but we expect him to-night."
was the reply. " Durrell and I came on a
few days before him."

" I return to Boston to-morrow," said
Choate, " and I should like to see Leo before
I go, if possible."

" If possible ? " repeated Less, " why, of

course it's possible. I'll tell you : I give a little supper to night, after the theatre, to Durrell and some of his company, we shall have Leo there, suppose you come too ? "

" Well, really. I—I—— " stammered Choate.

" It is to be simply a friendly gathering."

" I don't like to intrude."

" No intrusion, I assure you," said Less, " rather a pleasure. Come to Hayes' studio at eleven,—you know the place I think ? "

" Yes, indeed."

" All right ; I'll look for you. There's to be a jolly crowd of fellows, some of our best friends, you know, a sort of compliment to Leo."

" Very nice of you, I'm sure," said Choate, " I'll try to look in."

" Good ! " And the gentlemen parted.

" Great Scott ! " chuckled Less, as he watched Choate's departing figure. " What a joke ! It'll be rich to watch that old puri-

tan when he finds himself with Tiger Lily
and the rest of 'em ; a study for a picture,
by Jove ! "

And Choate smiled grimly, as he walked
away, muttering to himself, " It will be
strange if I cannot find a good foundation
to work upon to-night."

When Leo arrived in New York he was
met by Less and Durrell, who gave him hardly
time to dress before they hurried him to the
theatre to see the final scenes of a burlesque.
Here for the first time he saw Miss Laurence
Varney, otherwise Tiger Lily.

She was a magnificent woman, young,
tall, well-formed, with a light grace about
all her movements that quite banished the
impression that she was too large, which a
first glance might give rise to.   Her hair was
black and glossy, her eyes of the same color,
shaded by beautifully-arched brows and long
lashes, in sharp contrast to the clear olive

skin and ruddy lips, and even upon the stage she made use of very few devices to heighten her charms, in the exhibition of which she was by no means chary.

" Well, Leo, what do you think of her ? " asked Less.

" A beautiful woman," replied Leo, shortly.

" How would she do as a model for your Diana ? "

" She might, but that type of. woman is hardly——"

" Never mind the picture," interrupted Durrell, " How will she do for King Robert ? "

" Very well, provided she is capable of portraying a certain pathetic quality, which must mark the manner of the fool, even in his jests."

" And she can do it," said Durrell, " she's a mighty clever woman, sir. There's the last chorus. Come on." And the three men left the theatre.

Half an hour later they entered Hayes'

4

studio, where they met Hayes, Miss Varney, and three of her sister-actresses, Guida Estes, Cora Shirley and Alma Mandell, a trio of very pretty and lively young women, and a child, the little daughter of Guida Estes, who had acted in the play of the evening, figuring upon the programme as Little Ada. Less and Durrell were greeted familiarly by all, and Leo was introduced at once.

"Sorry if we kept you waiting," said Less, " but I shan't waste time with excuses, and if you're all ready we'll go in at once," and offering his arm to Guida he led the way to an adjoining room, where a tempting table was spread.

Leo offered his arm to Laurence Varney, the "Tiger Lily." He had been unaware, until he entered the room, that he was expected to make one of a midnight supper party; had he known it he would have made some excuse to stay away ; not because he deemed it wrong, or feared temptation, he

had often before made one at similar gather-
ings, but now, he thought, there was a pure
girl at home with whom he hoped soon to
link his life, and he felt that it would distress
and shock her to know he was in such company, that he owed it to his respect for her
to keep clear of all contaminating influences ;
still, finding himself placed as he was, he
could not well withdraw without offending
his friends, and perhaps sacrificing all chance
of gaining a hearing for his play, and so he
decided to remain, mentally determining
that it should be the last affair of its kind
for him.

"Come, Ada," said Tiger Lily kindly, to
the child who had been left alone, forgotten
by her mother. "You shall sit with this
gentleman and me."

The child came to Leo's side at once, "I
like you," she said decidedly.

Tiger Lily laughed. "You have made a
conquest already," she observed, "and no in-

considerable one, I assure you. Ada is very hard to win. I believe I am the only person in the company she obeys ; her own mother can do nothing with her.

Leo glanced at Guida, who was laughing and chatting with Less, utterly oblivious of her child, and then at the little one, standing demurely at his side. "I am sure she is a sweet-tempered child," he said, "her face shows it."

"Yes, indeed," answered Tiger Lily as they seated themselves at the table, "and there's an old head upon her little shoulders. I think she is misunderstood."

"Many of us are."

"Sometimes I think all are,—I am, I know; but it is because I am an actress, a burlesque actress, one who sells her beauty to the public gaze ; yet for all that I am a woman, with a woman's aims and ambitions."

"Which you may some day realize and enjoy," said Leo, sympathetically, touched by the tinge of pain which colored the actress's blunt words.

"Never. I have been guilty of the unpardonable sin ; I have sold my modesty. I have become a shameless *actress*, and am branded forever, for I am a woman. Were I a man I would have committed no transgression, but civilization has not yet reached the point where man and woman are equal, and, until it does, woman must suffer."

Leo was silent, he did not know how to answer this strange outburst. After a moment Tiger Lily laughed and continued, "I suppose you are wondering why I talk thus to you ? I don't know myself ; it's a whim, and I make it a point to gratify all my whims. I am a strange girl, they tell me. When the child expressed a liking for you at first sight, I felt confidence in you too, for I believe in the power of intuition which children are said to possess, and so——" she broke off abruptly, shrugged her shoulders,

and began to eat. Evidently she wished to
make him forget her words.

"Well, little one," said Leo, turning to
Ada, "what do you want?"

"Some charlotte russe, please, and a glass
of champagne."

"Surely," said Leo, turning to Tiger Lily,
"you do not give this child champagne?"

"Just a taste, that is all. Here, Ada, you
shall sip mine."

"She ought to be in bed, long ago."

"So she had, but children brought up on
the stage differ from the ordinary."

"I should say they did! Why, what can
be the future of a child who at her age at-
tends midnight champagne suppers?"

"And," continued Tiger Lily, feelingly,
"who nightly hears and sees the words and
sights that are the inevitable accompaniment
of a burlesque troupe. I have told Guida of
it often, but my words have no effect; the
child is clever, and earns a larger salary than

her mother does, and so she must grow up one of us. There is advanced civilization in a nutshell for you : everything from childhood to age, soul, body, conscience, all, to be had for money ; and there is no help for it."

" Little one," said Leo to the child, " you told me you liked me."

" Yes, I do."

" Then will you do something for me ?"

" What is it ?"

" Promise me that you will not drink any more champagne."

" Never ?"

" Never."

The child looked hesitatingly up into his face. " Will it please you very much ?" she asked at length.

" Very much."

" Then I will."

" Thank you, little one."

" But I don't see what difference it makes to you."

" It makes this difference, little one ; you like me, and I like you very much, and because I like you I don't want you to drink it, for it is not good for you."

" I suppose it don't hurt grown folks, does it ?" asked the child.

" If they drink much, it does."

"Then you must promise me not to drink much."

" I promise."

" And now make Tiger Lily promise."

" She will not drink much," said Leo, somewhat confusedly, while the actress laughed.

"But make her promise," insisted Ada. "I know she will, because she likes you."

" How do you know that, Ada ?" asked Tiger Lily.

" Because you talk to him like it."

A burst of laughter from the other members of the party interrupted them. Less, warming under the genial influence of the wine and the bright eyes about him was relating one

of his famous stories. " Well," he continued, "the only thing left for us to do was
to drive there. It was a bitter cold night,
and I wanted to wait until morning, but
nothing would suit Charlie but to drive over
at once. The supper had been a gorgeous
success and we started off, pretty well warmed
up with the wine we had been drinking.
We walked through a number of crooked
streets and almost lost ourselves, for we were
both strangers in the town, but at last we
struck a stable, where we hired a team,
promising to send it back in the morning.
By that time we were thoroughly chilled,
and Charlie insisted upon a warm drink before the drive, so we had some punch. He
bought a bottle of whiskey and took it into
the carriage. Every once in a while we took
a drop in order to keep ourselves warm.
Well, the consequence of mixing champagne,
rum-punch and whiskey is intoxication, and
we both succumbed to the consequences ; and

permit me to say, by way of parenthesis,
that I prefer as a stimulant to intoxication,
ever since then, an intangible something
which writers like my friend Leo there, call
bliss. Well, we both were so full of consequences, that we put up at the very first
hotel we struck, forgetting all about Charlie's
urgent business. The next morning we
woke to find ourselves ten miles further
from our destination than we were when we
started to drive; we had been going the
wrong way all the time, and the worst of it
was, *we had entirely forgotten where we
hired that team.* We drove back to the town
where we thought we had been the night before, but could find no trace of the owner.
Business compelled Charlie to follow the company, and we had to take that blasted horse
with us wherever we went. For a week
we paid his board, and took him from town
to town with us, and finally we were arrested
by the indignant owner as horse-thieves. It

cost us a pretty penny to get out of that scrape too, eh, Charlie?"

"But we did it," said Durrell laughing; "we generally land right side up."

"Come now," cried Less, "I've started the story-telling, who's next?"

No one answered.

" Here Leo," he continued, "You're a story-teller by trade, give us one now by way of a sample and we are not particular to have it a parable."

"My ability, such as it is," said Leo, as he saw all eyes turned towards him, "lies in story-writing, not telling, but I will do what I can. I was greatly amused at a very classical chamber concert which I attended in Boston, by an example of the far-famed 'Boston culture' which the comic papers use as a standing joke. The music was rendered by an excellent string orchestra, but the pro-gramme was so heavy that long before the last number the audience was thoroughly exhausted. This last number was to be the heaviest piece of all, and was supposed, according to the programme to represent in its various movements, sickness, delirium, exhaustion, rest, convalescence, and health." At the last moment it was thought advisable to substitute a well-known composition of Mozart's for this piece, in order to lighten the effect of the concert, and the change was made without informing the audience. I overheard a gentleman explaining the music as it progressed to the ladies he was escorting. He explained from his programme, finding the representation of sickness, delirium, et cetera, in Mozart's work with so much ingenuity that the great composer himself might have been persuaded that he had represented the themes set down upon the programme, although anything of so gloomy a nature was far from his thoughts when he composed the lively strains."

"That's a pretty flat story, Leo," volunteered Less, bluntly, "you can do better, come, try again, and give us something spicy."

"Later, perhaps," replied Leo, "give some one else a chance."

"Why do you feel under restraint with us?" asked Tiger Lily, turning to Leo.

"Under restraint? Why do you ask that? I assure you I am perfectly at ease."

"Yes, at ease as you would be in a drawing room or at a reception. Etiquette is hardly necessary here."

"How would you have me conduct myself?"

"I hardly know," answered Tiger Lily, "there is something in your manner that makes it appear as if you felt yourself out of place."

"Nonsense, I have attended many a Bohemian supper, in fact I am a thorough Bohemian, ask Less, if you doubt me."

"Oh, I believe you. You are a very odd

fellow, I think ; I've read a lot of those parables you write, and they confirm my belief. I'm an odd girl, too, and so I rather like you : I think we shall be friends."

"I hope so," murmured Leo. He felt a tugging at his coat sleeve and turning, saw that Ada wished to speak to him. " What is it, little one ? " he asked.

"I told you Tiger Lily liked you," said the child, triumphantly, "and now she says so herself ; you see I was right."

Leo raised his glass to his lips, at a loss for a reply.

"Little pitchers," laughed Tiger Lily, "I think," she continued, after a moment, "that I can find the key to your reserve."

Leo smiled. " Try it," he said.

" Are you in love ? " she asked bluntly.

" Yes," he answered, promptly.

" I don't believe it," said Tiger Lily smilingly, " you confess too freely."

" If I said no, you would not believe me,"

said Leo, good-naturedly, " and I said yes, and
you do not believe me. Perhaps I answered
as I do not wish you to believe."

She laughed.

"How did they come to call you Tiger
Lily !" he asked, to change the subject, for
he would have deemed it sacrilege to speak
of Rose in such company, and the conversation was too near her to please him.

"I rather like a nickname," replied Tiger
Lily, "and some one called me Tiger Lily
once, when I was angry, and the name has
clung to me. I shall keep it until I can find
a better. Can you suggest an improvement ?
you are an author, and ought to be able
to."

"Since you challenge me in that way I've
a mind to make the attempt, although I
hardly know you well enough to do so."

"Never mind, try it. Attention, everybody !" she called, raising her voice and rap-
ping upon the table. "My old nickname of

Tiger Lily is worn out, and our author is going to supply a new one."

Every one turned smilingly to Leo.

"Come, fire away, old man," cried Less, "we're all attention. Fill up everybody and drink to the christening."

The laughter and noise following this sally drowned the sound of a closing door as Oliver Choate entered the outer room. He saw, through the door, which stood ajar, the half-intoxicated men and women within, and Leo rising smilingly to say, as he held aloft a brimming glass of champagne, "Miss Laurence Varney, henceforth be it known to all whom it may concern, that we, the august Court of Nicknames, do solemnly decree, that on this, the twenty-ninth day of November, Anno Domino, Eighteen Hundred and Ninety-three, you shall cast aside for use upon state occasions, the nickname of Tiger Lily, and shall use the said name for rainy days only; and furthermore, be it decreed that the state nickname which you shall henceforward be known by is, Miss Larry."

"Miss Larry forever!" vociferated the company, as they rose to their feet and pledged the actress with brimming glasses.

Tiger Lily rose also with a pretence of emotion and said tremulously, "Friends, this enthusiasm is too much, I am quite overcome, believe me I—I—ah, Godpapa, support me?" and with mock faintness she threw herself into Leo's arms.

The company burst into a roar of laughter and drained their glasses. Oliver Choate turned from the scene, and beckoning a servant who was passing said to him, "Take my card to Mr. Ingraham, and tell him I regret that I cannot stop," and he left the place hurriedly, chuckling to himself as he went, "I've got him!" he muttered gleefully, "I've got him now!"

5

CHAPTER IV.

THE PARTING.

.

"Parting is such sweet sorrow
That I could say good-night, till it be morrow."
SHAKSPERE (*Romeo and Juliet*).

AFTER reading Leo's play, Durrell's stage-manager, a man old and experienced in his business, shook his head dubiously, saying, "It's an excellent work, too good for us, that's the trouble. It may go; still, before reading it to the company, I would advise a few further alterations. When they hear it they will ask for more changes, you may be sure, but what I advise will be absolutely necessary before the piece can be produced."

And so Leo set to work with a will, rewriting as he was directed, working with all the more vigor because he knew his task must be finished before he could return to Rose. For nearly a week he applied himself steadily, and during this time did not hear a word from home. He wrote several times to Rose but received no answer, and it was with a feeling of relief that he at length completed his task and announced his readiness to read the work to Durrell and his company.

Both Durrell and Less tried repeatedly to induce him to join them in supping with the actresses or in wandering about the city in search of adventures, and exploring some of its most questionable quarters, but he was firm in his refusals, much to the chagrin of Less, who had counted upon his company in their escapades. Leo felt that an explanation was due to his friend, and he confided to him the fact of his love for Rose and his hopes of winning her. Less appreciated the motives which prompted the refusals, and said nothing further to weaken Leo's resolve.

Leo often met little Ada and the ladies of Durrell's company. The child had taken a great liking to him, and insisted upon calling upon him frequently. Her mother refused to take her, but Tiger Lily volunteered to humor her whim, and brought her to his hotel nearly every day, led not so much by the child's caprice as by a strong inclination of her own.

When he left her, on the night of the supper, Leo was inclined to think that Tiger Lily was as common as most of the women whom Less chose to associate with, but the more he saw of her, the more he was forced to alter his opinion. True, she was lax in her morals, but this, he came to think, was more the result of association than of choice; there was a refinement about her that the others lacked; a womanliness not yet destroyed by her fast life. She told him her story. Her mother died in giving her birth, and her father had brought her up sur-

rounded with every luxury that wealth could
secure, until her fourteenth year, when
a great financial panic swallowed up his
entire fortune, and he, rather than face the
penury that awaited him, committed suicide.
The girl was compelled to leave the palatial
home to which she had been accustomed all
her life, and go to live with some distant
relatives of her father's in a remote country
town. Her guardians were narrow-minded
people of limited means, who felt that they
were doing a great charity by adopting the
child, and they let her know it. She was no
longer petted and waited upon, in fact, she
was looked upon as a sort of upper-servant ;
and while her duties were not hard, still they
were galling after her past life, and she was
thoroughly miserable. Her guardians were
not unkind, but too uncultivated to understand her and they constantly reproached her
for her weeping and ungratefulness while
they extolled their own virtue in charitably

harboring her. For several months she bore
her lot, if not patiently, at least without com-
plaint, but the fires of rebellion smouldered
in her breast ready to flare up at any moment.

Her greatest passion had always been
for the stage, and her father, whose
tastes had been similar, encouraged her ;
but her guardians were of the strictest
puritan type and regarded the stage as a
snare of Satan, avoiding shows and show
people as a pestilence, and forbidding her
to have anything to do with them. It
happened that several members of a
third-rate burlesque troupe came to the
village to pass a few summer weeks, and
Tiger Lily made their acquaintance. The
manager of the troupe, a shrewd young
fellow, heard her sing and saw that she
had ability of no mean order. As days
passed, they became very friendly, and when
—to amuse themselves—the company gave
a performance in the Town Hall, Tiger

Lily received tickets. Her guardians, however, forbade her attending, and furthermore told her that she must never again
associate with her new-found friends.
She did not answer, but when the evening
of the performance came, stole from the
house and went. The next day there was a
scene, and her long pent-up wrath ex-
ploded. Her guardians stormed and finally
one of them struck her. It was the first
blow she had ever received and she was
almost delirious with anger. That night
she left her home forever, flying to her
theatrical friends. She was given a position in the company and for a time fared
well, but she was beautiful, she was innocent, she was but a child and her associates
were thoroughly unscrupulous ; her surroundings tended to blunt her moral per-
ceptions, and her very innocence caused her
downfall. A brute took advantage of her
youth, and before she was a woman she

was—oh, the pity of it!—one of the fallen. Think of it, you who know what this means!—she, poor child, did not, she but followed in the footsteps of her companions, she was conscious of no wrong—but the consciousness came with womanhood and with it the knowledge of the impotency of regret and repentance. She left her old companions to join Durrell and his company, but, while the change was greatly for the better, she had not freed herself from the old life, nor could she ever, try as she might. There were times when she sought oblivion in the wine-cup, desperate in her sorrow, but there always came the reaction. She had taken her place and must abide by her choice through life; there was no alternative, rebel as she might. The mud of the roadway clings forever about a woman's skirts, but scarcely soils the garments of a man.

The knowledge of all this softened Leo, and

he treated her with a kindly consideration and respect that drew her unconsciously towards him. Her woman's heart yearned for sympathy and he gave it to her, and then her yearning grew into love. He was blind to her infatuation, and only saw in her an object for sympathy and a beautiful woman whom he hoped to paint in a picture that would make him famous.

On the morning of the last day of the company's engagement in New York, Leo read his manuscript before them all. Little was said before him in praise or dispraise of the play, and he left them to discuss their impressions, stating, however, that he proposed leaving for Boston on the night express.

Durrell called upon him later in the day, bringing the verdict of his players. "The piece is all right," he said, "but the burlesque is hardly broad enough; introduce a couple of topical songs, some

chances for skirt dancing, and for horse-
play by the comedians and it will go ; "
and turning over the leaves of the manuscript, he gave some examples of what he
meant.

"But, my dear Durrell," cried Leo,
"don't you see that my subject is one
requiring the utmost delicacy to burlesque ?
Such broad bits of humor as you suggest,
while they may be very well in their way,
are entirely out of place in a piece like
'King Robert.'"

"Yes, yes, that's all very well from a
literary standpoint," answered Durrell ;
"but people who go to see a burlesque
are seldom literary, and their palates are
not educated to appreciate a delicate
flavor, they must have something with a
tang, and what they demand I must
supply."

"Well," replied Leo, decidedly, "in
that case you are not to be blamed, of

course, but I do not think I can suit
such tastes. If my work cannot be presented as it was conceived, I do not think
I care to have it done at all. You have
a public to please whose tastes you must
observe, but I, on the other hand, have a
reputation as a writer to maintain which
will not permit me to lower the standard of
my work by writing what you require."

" Tut, tut !" cried Durrell, "what's the
use of splitting hairs. If you don't wish it
known that you are the author of the piece,
use a *nom-de-plume*. The price we have
agreed upon is larger than *Hermes* pays
for ten times the work there is in the play,
and as for your standard, keep it up in the
paper."

" There is a great deal in having one's
ideas correctly presented, Durrell," answered
Leo, " and you want to distort mine into a
caricature of what they really are ; and as
they are but caricatures originally, you are

striving to make a caricature of a caricature :
just think what an abortion that would
be."

" You are altogether too nice in your
ideas," snapped Durrell, impatiently.

" Perhaps I am, and I will not decide on
this thing now. Give me a little time to
think it over."

" Very well, I'll see you in Boston next
week. You know we close here to-night and
leave for Boston to-morrow and lay over
there a day or two. I sold out a few days'
time here to an amateur company. We
play through New England for the next two
weeks, and you and I can meet and settle
matters before the company goes west."

"So be it."

"By the way, Leo, why don't you wait
over until to-morrow and travel with us ?
See how it storms."

" I can't," replied Leo, thinking of Rose.
"I've stayed here longer than I ought to

now; I have something to attend to which I do not like to put off."

"Business comes first, of course. Well, till we meet again," and with a hearty hand-shake, Durrell took his leave.

Half an hour later Tiger Lily called with little Ada.

" Ada insisted we should call again before you left, and here we are," said Tiger Lily, as she entered.

"And you are both welcome, he replied heartily. "How is the little one to-day ?"

"I'm nicely," said Ada, perching herself upon his knee. " You ought to feel flattered at our coming to see you through all this storm."

"Indeed I am, little one, highly flat-tered."

"I like you to call me ' little one,' it's so much nicer than Ada."

" Do you think so ?"

"Yes. I think you've got a special knack

about nicknames; now you call Tiger Lily, Miss Larry, and she likes it too."

"How do you know that, Ada?" asked Tiger Lily with a smile.

"'Cause you laugh when anybody calls you it. Say," she continued, turning again to Leo, "are you going away to-day, truly?"

"Truly."

"Won't we see you any more?"

"Oh, yes, I hope so."

"When?"

"Perhaps next week."

"Well, I'm glad, 'cause I thought maybe we wouldn't, and it's hard on a person to lose old friends, and we are old friends, ain't we?"

"Yes, indeed, very old friends, little one. I've loved the girls ever since I learned to talk; I love them now, and you are one of the most favored ones," and with a merry laugh Leo kissed the child's upturned face.

Tiger Lily watched them wistfully and sighed.

"A penny for your thoughts, Miss Larry!" he cried. "What lucky swain caused that sigh? Here, little one," he continued, detaching a tiny gold charm from his watch-chain, "wear this on your necklace, to remember me by."

"Oh, thank you, I'm ever so much obliged," cried the child delightedly, as she took the little gift. "I don't need anything to remember you by, but still, I shall like something to keep, you have given me."

"What an interest you take in the child," observed Tiger Lily.

"Well, you see she takes a great interest in me, and I only reciprocate," laughed Leo.

"Can I look at your pictures, please?" interrupted Ada, gathering up an armful of illustrated papers and magazines.

"Certainly, little one, take them over to the window where it is lightest."

"You do not always reciprocate such an interest," said Tiger Lily absently.

"Why do you say that?"

"Do you think you do?"

"I hope I am not ungrateful."

"No, not that."

"What then?"

"I sometimes think you are strangely unobservant for one who writes and paints, and who is consequently ever on the watch for little traits of character and tricks of expression," she said, in the same absent, dreamy way. "People's motives, and sometimes their thoughts, ought to be more apparent to you than to others."

"I can be blinded as well as another," he said, with a puzzled frown.

"Did you never think that you may be blind yourself?" she asked with a far-away look.

"I do not understand you."

She sighed, and said, "Perhaps it is as well that you do not."

"I sometimes think that you do not understand yourself," cried Leo, impetuously. "You were not born for such a life as you lead ; you have a sympathetic heart, a womanliness, that unfits you for it. It is suited only to women like Ada's mother, selfish, callous creatures, with no aim higher than self-indulgence. You could make some man happy ; Guida never could."

"I could make some man happy ? Maybe, I cannot say, but could some man make me happy ?" murmured Tiger Lily, tremulously.

"I think so, if I read you rightly; but you have just said that I do not read character well, so perhaps that is hardly for me to say ; it would all depend upon yourself."

Tiger Lily was agitated ; she was pale, and her hands trembled as she toyed with the fringe upon her chair. There was a
6

tremor in her voice as she replied. "Not all, I might try, but my success would depend largely upon what manner of man he was. Oh, Leo, if he were like you, dear—" she paused suddenly, checked by an instant realization of what her impetuosity had hurried her into saying and covered her face with her hands.

Leo rose to his feet with an exclamation of surprise and pain. He glanced towards Ada to see if the child had heard the actress's words and saw that she was deep in picture-land, utterly oblivious of what was going on around her.

"Miss Varney," he said, after a painful pause, "when I return home I shall be engaged to a young girl whom I love with all my heart :"

"Oh !" she exclaimed passionately, "please forget what I have said, I did not mean to tell you, I—I—Oh, I am bad enough, Heaven knows, but I have not sunk to——"

" Ah, Miss Larry," he said kindly, touched by her distress, "I may have been blind to some things, as you say, but I think I have read you well, after all, believe me, your words have not changed my good opinion of you."

" We shall see little of each other hereafter," she said, bitterly; "a good thing, too, —but—but—you will always be my friend ? "

" I will try."

" And—she—tell me about her."

" We have been companions from childhood," he replied, "she is good, beautiful, innocent as Heaven, and she loves me."

" How his love for her is written on his very face," thought Tiger Lily, as she watched him wistfully. "What is her name ?" she asked.

" Rose."

" I release you from your promise."

" What promise ? "

" To be my friend," she answered, sadly.

"If you wed her you cannot keep it. She is pure and innocent, you say, therefore she cannot be my friend ; as her husband you cannot associate with a burlesque actress without causing comment, perhaps jealousy on her part, and consequent unhappiness to yourself and this I will not have. Come Ada, we must go."

"You are too good a woman for the place you fill," said Leo earnestly.

" I have fallen in the mire and the stain is indelible. Good-bye, Leo," she said tearfully, " God bless and prosper you."

" Good-bye, Miss Larry, believe me, I am your friend at heart, and—and I feel for you. Good-bye, little one," and he stooped to kiss the child and hide his face.

Tiger Lily laughed bitterly and said, " Were I other than I am I should have deserved more than your pity, but as it is— Good-bye," and she was gone with the child.

For a long time Leo sat thinking, after

their departure and then, with an impatient sigh, he began to write a parable for *Hermes*, seeking to distract his thoughts by work. And he wrote thus :

" Long, long ago lived a race of men called the Humanii, famed far and wide for their beauty, their nobility of character and their moral purity. For years they dwelt happily in a fair and fertile valley and were the favored of the Gods until a great man of their race, Athea, by name, defied the Gods and the people upheld him.

" To punish the Humanii for their rebellion the Gods created a monster, half man, half beast, called the Lustous that for a long time mercilessly ravaged the country and slew the people, despite their resistance. Their utmost efforts were hopeless, for the monster was so terrible that his very appearance deprived the bravest of courage. After a time a treaty was made with the Lustous, whereby the monster agreed to cease his work of devastation provided the Humanii sent to him as a sacrifice, at stated intervals, the most beautiful maiden of their nation.

" Eve was the first selected, and she set forth amid the cries and wailings of a great concourse, for she was as fair and pure as the new-fallen snow and, even in her great fear, a blush came to her cheeks when she found herself the centre of so much attention, and she modestly cast down her eyes. The escort that accompanied her to the Lustous mountain den came back without her, in silence and sorrow.

" And time rolled on until it was necessary to find a second sacrifice for the monster and Thais was the maiden selected. At the foot of the hills, where dwelt the Lustous, Thais and her escort met Eve, the first sacrifice, who laughed and said to her weeping successor, 'Weep not, no harm will befall thee, and when another comes to take thy place thou wilt return as I do.'

" When Eve returned with the escort, a great crowd gathered about them, shouting with joy that the beautiful maid was returned to them. She did not blush and cast down her eyes, as when she left her home, but rather invited the gaze of the multitude upon her charms, and laughed and chatted with the men. She was the same, yet changed, her beauty, which had before been cloaked with modesty now assumed a garb of boldness. Many men sought her company, and in these men evil traits, before unknown among the Humanii, began to appear.

"And by and by, Thais returned and another maid went forth to the den of the Lustous and Eve and Thais were much together, and they beguiled other maidens to be of their company, teaching them to assume the unblushing manners which they had learned. For those who were thus taught there was no change; if once they entered upon the ways of the monster his ways must, perforce, be their ways thenceforward, forever. And all the men and women who were followers of Eve and Thais began to develop evil traits unknown before.

"In time the number of maidens who had been to the monster's den increased, and as their number grew, so did their following until the Humanii became a tainted race. So low did this once noble people fall that the Lustous himself was summoned to rule the land, and they cast aside their name Humanii and called themselves the Lustii, in honor of their new ruler, and the women who had been sent to the den of the monster were raised to a high rank and called Wantons.

Cycles of years have passed, and the race of the Humanii has disappeared, yet the descendants of the Wantons still work ill to mankind, as the monster taught their ancestresses, ages ago, but they know not their origin.

CHAPTER V.

THE BLOOM AND THE SERE.

" Who wisely weds in his maturer years
Then let him choose a damsel young and fair
To bless his age."

PoPE   (*January and May*).

UPON his return to Boston, Oliver Choate found Mrs. Maynard again suffering from her old trouble, greatly to the alarm of Rose, who until then had no idea of the nature of her mother's ailment ; Mrs. Maynard soon rallied, however, but the doctor cautioned her very particularly to beware of any excitement or strong emotion.

Choate was kind and attentive in the extreme, and especially was he gentle to Rose, towards whom he showed a tender commiseration that she was shrewd enough to thoroughly understand.　One evening, as she sat with her mother and Choate, a letter was brought to her ; excusing herself, she eagerly opened it, and the older people, with very different emotions, noticed the smile and blush with which she read it.　Shortly afterwards she left the room, saying as she went, "Leo sends his regards."

Mrs. Maynard turned to Choate with a smile and said, "It is not hard to see how matters stand between the young people."

Oliver Choate scowled, bit his lips, and abruptly left the room.

He followed the young girl, and confronting her abruptly, exclaimed, "Rose, I want to have an understanding with you."

The girl started and changed color, "About what ?" she asked hypocritically.

"You know well enough ; I want you to choose here and now between Leo Ormsby and me ; between the man who can offer you a life of economy, such as you have always

led, and one who offers you a palace and all
that wealth can buy."

"You—I—you are very abrupt."

"I make you a simple proposition, Rose,
we will not discuss sentiment now, will you
choose a genteel pittance or affluence ? You
know that Leo is unable to give you more
than you have, and if you are content with
that we will say no more about it." He
paused, tremblingly awaiting her reply.

" Oh, I hate economy, I hate it !" she exclaimed fiercely.

" Then marry me."

" But Leo——"

" Are you betrothed to him ?"

" No, but——"

" Then follow your best judgment ; I know
you prefer the younger man's love and the
old man's wealth, but you may not have
both. Believe me, I will be a good
husband ; there is nothing I would not do for
you——"

"Oh!" exclaimed Rose, "mother would never hear of it!"

"Let me try to win her consent, I am sure I can."

"I am not so sure; Leo is her prime favorite; besides, I do not know but what I prefer him myself."

"I can understand that it is hard for you to decide, my dear; let your mother do so for you. I will state the case to her, bluntly, and we will abide by her verdict."

"Speak to her, if you will," said Rose, as she turned to leave him, "but I do not promise anything."

"I win!" muttered Choate exultantly.

He returned to Mrs. Maynard at once, and spoke of Leo and Rose.

"They will be betrothed soon. I think," smilingly declared the widow.

"Then you look for serious results?" he inquired.

"Why, Oliver, I am not blind, and surely

you must have seen," exclaimed Mrs. Maynard, in surprise.

"Yes, yes, of course," he assented, "and
do you approve?"

"You know I do, heartily. It seems to
me that you are speaking very differently
from your usual tone ; has anything occurred
to change you?"

"Yes, Mrs. Maynard, something has occurred which I deem it my duty to tell you
before it is too late.

"Too late?"

"Yes. Consideration for your health has
silenced me until now, but the time has
come when I must speak. You know the
character of Lester Ingraham, Leo's friend,
a man whose chosen society is the *demi-
monde*, and you have often heard me ask Leo
to give him up."

"Yes, yes."

"Ingraham is good-hearted enough, perhaps, but not the man one would select as a

husband for one's daughter. I am sorry to say, Mrs. Maynard, that I have every reason to believe that Leo is one of the same stamp."

"Why—we never saw an indication—you must be mistaken—what makes you think so?"

"I have the best, the strongest, proofs; believe me, I would not thus pain you otherwise. I was invited by Ingraham to a midnight supper in New York. It was the very night that Leo arrived there, direct from Rose. I went to this supper and saw through the open door—for I did not enter the supperroom, nor did the people there see me,—I saw Leo with his friends, seated at the table with a number of women. Leo rose, glass in hand, and toasted one of these creatures, and she, while they drank her health, rose also, and threw herself into his arms. I did not stay to see more. And this was on the very night he had left Rose, perhaps with kisses from her pure lips upon his, to go thus to one—

I think I need say no more; you know me of old. I am, I have proven that I am your friend, and I cannot tell you how it pains me to be the bearer of such evil news, but it is true."

Mrs. Maynard was ghastly. "God help us all! Oliver, I believe you," she cried piteously, "What shall I do? what shall I do?"

"I can hardly counsel you," he answered sadly, but with a fierce inward exultation.

"It will break her heart, it will break her heart," muttered Mrs. Maynard, rising and pacing unsteadily up and down the room, "Oliver, you must find a way out of it all, you must; it is too terrible! I want to feel that my girl's happiness, that her future, will be secure when I am gone. What's to be done? what's to be done?"

"Calm yourself," said Choate apprehensively, thinking of the doctor's warning and fearful of the consequences of such violent agitation, "this excitement will do you no good. Let us face the difficulty calmly and rationally. Here, be seated : " and he pushed a chair towards her.

"Never mind me, let us think of Rose, she is the one with suffering before her, I—Oh ! " she suddenly cried out, staggering blindly, "I—I think I will sit—the chair—the chair —quick ! "

Choate assisted her to a seat and bent anxiously over her. She held her hand, tightly clenched, over her heart, and after a moment, gasped painfully, " Do not alarm Rose. I— I am very ill again—must go to my room— call doctor—not Rose—Oh ! "

Throughout the night the household was in a state of suspense. Dr. Farnsworth labored tirelessly over the sick woman, but with little effect, and reluctantly, at length, he told the anxious ones that she had but a few hours to live.

Rose was led from the sick-room in a help-less agony of grief, but the invalid bore the news bravely.

The doctor had conquered her pain, and she was in comparative ease when she earnestly asked to be left alone with Oliver Choate and a clergyman who had been called in. For half an hour or more the three were closeted together, the indistinct murmur of their voices, now and then audible in the hall, being the only sign that death had not yet claimed his victim.

When Rose had sufficiently subdued her emotion she returned to her mother's room to wait before the door, with Doctor Farns-worth and the awe-stricken servant-maid, until she could enter, to look again, for the last time in life, upon the dear, kindly face that had smiled with her joy, wept with her sorrow, and been always by with ready sym pathy. There is no love like mother's love, and the thought that she was about to lose it

brought to Rose a stronger realization of its
value. All the sharp, unfilial words that
had ever passed her lips now returned to her
memory with startling distinctness. Why
had she not been a better child ? If she only
might live the past few years again,—if time
would but roll back ! But time inexorably
rolled on, bringing nearer, with each tick of
the clock, the moment of parting.

Doctor Farnsworth was all kindness and
consideration, but he knew, from long famil-
iarity with such scenes, that all efforts to
comfort the girl were useless, and he did
not try to check her passionate grief.

At length, after what seemed an intermi-
nable time, the door opened and Rose was
called.

"Control yourself, my child," whispered
the doctor, "for your mother's sake."

With a mighty effort, Rose forced back her
tears and entered the room ; but no sooner did
she behold the dying woman than all her

fortitude forsook her, and she sank beside the bed, hiding her face in the coverlet as she sobbed, "Mother, oh, mother !"

Mrs. Maynard laid her hand tenderly upon the bowed head of the grief-stricken girl, saying, "All is for the best, Rose ; God's will be done."

Oliver Choate raised the girl and said with very evident emotion : "Rose, your mother has something to say to you, and you must control yourself to listen. I know it is all very hard, but you must bear up. She is very weak and must not tax her strength too far, so listen, child, listen to her, it is for your own good."

Rose dried her eyes mechanically, and assuming a kneeling posture, took her mother's hand in both of hers, and said, with a sob, "What is it, mother, dear ?"

"Rose, I am thinking of your future."

"Don't think of me, mother."

"I must, my darling ; listen."

" Yes, dear," sobbed Rose, but her thoughts stumbled blindly after her mother's words ; she hardly followed their meaning, so dazed was she by the suddenness of the blow which was falling.

"I shall leave you penniless.   Mr. Choate offers you a home: I want you to accept it."

"I will, mother, gratefully."

" That is not all.   If you live in his house evil tongues will slander you, you must give him the right to protect you.   You must become his wife.   Will you ?"

" Mother, if you wish it," replied Rose.

"I want to see you his wife before I die." Another outburst of grief from Rose interrupted the dying woman, but in a moment it was controlled.   " I want you to be married, here, now, by my bedside."

"Mother, this is no time, no place."

" I wish it, Rose."

"Yes, mother."

"Mr. Lorrimer is here; he can perform the ceremony."

"Oh, mother!" sobbed the girl frantically.

"Call Dr. Farnsworth and Margaret, they can be witnesses."

Weeping bitterly Rose obeyed. While she was away from the bedside Choate bent over the invalid, who whispered solemnly, "She is saved from him. I trust you, Oliver; you must be very good to her."

He turned away trembling, his face ashy pale and convulsed with emotion, "Dying!" he muttered to himself, "surely it was not murder! I did not mean that my trick should——" he checked himself suddenly and peered at the others from under his brows to assure himself they had not heard his words.

Rose returned with the doctor and the servant, and held the dying woman's hand while the Reverend Mr. Lorrimer spoke the impressive words that bound her forever to Oliver Choate.

"Will you have this man to be your wedded husband, to live together after God's ordinance in the holy estate of matrimony, to love, honor and keep him, in sickness and in health and forsaking all others, keep thee only unto him so long as you both shall live?"

Her "yes" was spoken almost unconsciously. And Choate responded with none of the exultation he had dreamed of; guilt oppressed his conscience, and conscience destroyed his passion.

When the minister had duly pronounced them man and wife, Mrs. Maynard gave a great sigh and murmured, "Now I am at peace."

Dr. Farnsworth hurried to the bedside and bent over the invalid. In a moment he stood erect and, taking Rose by the hand, he said sadly and sympathetically, "It is all over, Mrs. Choate."

Rose stood dazed. All over? Her mother gone? Mrs. Choate? She was married and in a few days Leo would return. Leo! She had not thought of him, and now she was alone, all alone, she might not even turn to him for sympathy. She looked wildly about, from one to another. Her husband approached to comfort her, but she saw the doctor draw the sheet over that dear, still, smiling face on the bed, and with a wild hysterical laugh, fainted.

CHAPTER VI.

A BITTER HOME-COMING.

"But there where I had garnered up my heart,
Where either I must live or bear no life,
The fountain from the which my current runs,
Or else dries up ; to be discarded thence !"
                                    SHAKSPERE (*Othello*).

WITH a joyful elation that prompted him
to hum merrily, to whistle, to drum with his
fingers and express his feelings by many
little outward signs, Leo took the night
train for Boston. Snugly cased in a dainty
satin box in his pocket, he carried a ring, in
which glittered a diamond of great brilliancy, for Rose. The ring that was to finally
bind them together forever, in the harmony
of souls which is so perfect a mingling that
one only seems to exist ; the bond of love

which makes the true marriage. That which
is said before the altar is but the outward
evidence, the proclaiming to the world of
what has already happened within.

The weather was bad. For two or three
days it had been raining heavily, and there
was still no sign of clearing. The wind
rushed wildly by the flying train, dashing
the raindrops with a swift vicious patter
against the window panes, but Leo gave no
heed to the weather, his thoughts were in
Boston and his impatience to reach home
and Rose was almost unbearable. The moments seemed to drag interminably. He
threw away his half-smoked cigar and sought
his berth in the sleeper, thinking to pass the
hours in sleep. For a long time he tossed
restlessly, but at length the unceasing,
monotonous rumble of the train lulled his
tired senses to rest.

He was awakened by the shrill, piercing
shriek of the locomotive's whistle and the

jarring of the brakes, turned on suddenly, with full force to stop the train. All was confusion in the car, at once, and, unable to ascertain the cause of the trouble from any one about him, Leo hurriedly dressed and went out. The rain was still pouring in torrents and the night was inky black. Turning up his coat collar with a shudder and pulling his cap over his ears, he stepped from the car platform to the ground. A splash and spatter told him he had landed in a puddle. Here and there he could see the glimmer of some trainman's lantern which with the long row of lights from the windows of the motionless train, were the only spots that broke the blackness of the night. He walked forward to the locomotive, and, in the circle of light cast by the engine fires, found the conductor surrounded by about a dozen men.

"It's too dark to see just how bad it is," the conductor was saying, "and we'll have to lay over for an hour or two, and wait for daylight. 'Twouldn't be worth while now to go back, till we find out how we stand an' I wouldn't dare, anyhow. I don't know what other trains may be behind, an' I won't run no risk. A washout's bad enough without a smashup."

" Where are we ? " asked a passenger.

" In the meanest place on the road. Not a town anywhere near, and a nice thick woods all around us."

" That's pleasant."

" Wal, I'll git ye out of it quick's I can. I've sent back to telegraph for help ; that's all I can do now."

"The more hurry the less speed," muttered Leo ruefully as he tramped back, through mud and rain, to his place on the train.

Day dawned and the outlook was gloomy in the extreme. The rain still poured, and there was little prospect of the track being repaired for some hours. With several others, Leo undertook to walk to a village some two miles distant, and with much diffi- culty they reached the place, hired a team and drove to the nearest railway station on the other side of the washout. It was an out-of- the-way spot and they were compelled to wait a weary time for a train which they found, after all, did not make connections, and left them to wait again at another dreary country depot. It was nine o'clock that night when Leo reached Boston, tired, dirty, and hungry, but full of delight to think that he was once more near Rose.

He jumped into a hack and was driven di- rectly to the dear, familiar house. He ran lightly up the steps and pulled the bell vigor- ously. A terrific peal was the result of his exertion and he laughed aloud at the noise. The servant maid opened the door and he stepped in.

" Hullo, Margaret," he cried cheerily as he

removed his coat, how are they all? Well,
I suppose?"

"Oh, Mr. Leo," she said, with a stupid,
frightened look.

"Well, what's wrong? What makes you
stare at me like that? Is Rose——"

"It's Mrs. Maynard, sir."

"What, another of her attacks? Poor
lady!"

"She's dead, sir.'

"What?"

"Yes, sir, and buried."

"Good Heavens!"

"And—and Miss Rose——"

"Is she well, is she well? Speak, girl!"

"Yes, sir."

"My poor, poor girl! Where is she?"

"In the sitting-room, sir."

"This is awful. I'll go to her at once, as
I am. Take my valise to my room, please."
He made his way to the sitting-room and
found Rose alone. She did not see him but

sat, absorbed in thought, gazing intently into the fire that flashed and crackled on the hearth. There was a sadness in her posture that her mourning garb served to heighten, and Leo's heart thrilled with pity for her.

"Rose," he said softly.

With a little cry of terror she clutched the arms of her chair and turned a pallid face to him that showed traces of much weeping and care in the dark circles under the bloodshot eyes. "You, Leo!" she gasped.

"Yes, dear, it is I. Do not rise. Why did you not write me of your great sorrow that I might come to comfort you?"

"I—I—Oh, Leo!" a burst of tears choked her utterance.

"There, there, dear, never mind, I can quite understand that at such a time you could not think. I am here now and I know all, so I can help you to bear it. Now don't cry any more, be a brave little woman," and he drew up a chair and seated himself by her side.

"No, Leo, you don't know all, I—I——"

"But I do," he interrupted, "you are left penniless, eh? Well, what of that? I have enough for two, and you shall share with me. You knew all along that you were to be my wife, didn't you, dear? and this misfortune only binds us closer together. Why, I brought the ring for you from New York, see, isn't it a beauty?" and he took the little satin box from his pocket.

"Put it away, put it away!" cried Rose, almost inarticulately as she turned away from him to hide her face.

"Pardon me, dear," he said, as he obeyed her "it was wrong and selfish of me to bring it forth at such a time, but my heart——"

"Mr. Ormsby, I forbid you to speak so to me," said Rose, with an effort. How she despised herself as she spoke and how noble he seemed, how gentle, how full of tender sympathy, but she must end it all, she must, at once and forever.

Leo looked at her in surprise, but her pale, sad face, her gloomy dress, and her evident agitation filled him with pity and he replied gently, "As you please."

"I must also request that you find another lodging. I need your room."

Leo smiled. "That is all right enough," he replied. "At present it is hardly proper that I should remain here, but by-and-by——"

She rose to her feet tremblingly, and choked back a sob. With a miserable effort to appear dignified she half whispered, "My husband wishes it," and then sank back into her chair, sobbing uncontrollably.

Leo started up with an exclamation of dismay : "My dear child, you are ill," he cried.

"No," she sobbed wildly, "I am married."

For a moment he stood looking at her in unbelief, but her distress served to convince him that there was more in her words than he had supposed. He felt a great heart-sickness creep over him, and became so giddy that he was forced to grasp a chair for support. Rose remained seated, now and then uttering a sob under the handkerchief which hid her face, utterly miserable.

"I will not believe it!" gasped Leo, at length. He was very pale and trembled violently.

The sound of a footstep attracted his notice, and, turning, he saw Oliver Choate entering the room. "Ah, Mr. Choate," he cried, advancing to meet the new-comer, with extended hand, "you are my friend; tell me, she is unwell, it is untrue!"

Oliver Choate ignored Leo's proffered hand and crossed the room to where Rose sat, "I do not know what you refer to, sir," he said coldly; "but my wife is as well as

8

can be expected after her late bereavement."

"Your wife? Oh, my God, my God!" exclaimed Leo, sinking into a chair and covering his face. For several moments perfect silence reigned, and the ticking of the clock on the mantle, only, was heard.

"Rose dear," said Choate, at last, "this is too much for you. Leave us here, alone," and he laid his hand tenderly upon her shoulder.

She shook him off roughly, saying with fierce bitterness, "do not touch me!"

Leo rose. "Do not," he said ironically, while his voice trembled strangely, "do not let me be the cause of a quarrel, especially during the delightful days of your honeymoon. I will go."

"Stay, sir," said Choate as Leo turned to leave the room, "this will probably be our last meeting, and there are some things which you may wish explained."

"I ask no explanation. It is enough for me that the lady has preferred your riper years and maturer charms to my youth and inexperience," replied Leo, sarcastically.

"Rose, will you leave us?" said Choate.

"No!" she answered decidedly.

"As you please," he returned with a shrug of his shoulders.

"Leo," cried Rose, suddenly with passionate earnestness, "at my mother's death-bed I married this man because she bade me, and I did not think of myself or of—of any one. It was not love—oh, no—you cannot think that—oh, I am so miserable!"

"And I," said Choate, determined to bring matters to an end now, once and for all, "knowing exactly how matters stood, allowed it to go on—something I would never have done had I not seen a certain midnight supper in New York where you and your chosen friend, Ingraham, regaled a choice assembly of loose women. I saw one

of them in your arms, sir, and that on the
very day you had left Rose, with protesta-
tions of love.   The sight convinced me that
you were not fit a husband for her, and I
married her to save her from you."

"You do not understand—" began Leo.

"Pardon me."

"By the almighty God," he cried, despairingly, "on my soul, I am as innocent as she
is!"

Rose sobbed bitterly.

"It is too late to protest now," said
Choate, "if an error has been made, it must
be abided by.   I had the evidence of my
eyes and ears."

"Believe me 'or not, as you will," said
Leo, bitterly, "it matters little now."

"I believe you," cried Rose hysterically,
"I believe you, Leo."

"It is a pity you allowed your belief to
be shaken at all," he returned contemptuously.   "Do you know what it is you have

done ? You were to me the embodiment of everything that is true, trusting, noble—my ideal ; but you have shattered that bright dream and left me alone in darkness, a poor wreck, stranded upon a desert, with no one to turn to, no one to trust. You thrust me forth from the home-life which you hold up to me as an example to go—to theDevil, per-haps."

Rose did not answer, but her sobs re-doubled.

"All this is useless, Mr. Ormsby," said Choate, "useless and cruel. Don't you see how agitated Rose is? Have you no thought for any one besides yourself ?"

"I am going, sir," said Leo, with a scorn-ful laugh, "good-bye, Mrs. Choate. I wish you much happiness," and he left the room.

Choate turned to his wife, who had risen to her feet, and was moving unsteadily across the room. He approached to support

her, and the sound of the closing door that
shut Leo from the house reached his ears.

Rose heard it too, and turned a wild,
furious look upon him as she hissed, "you
tricked me, by my mother's death-bed, you
tricked me into becoming your wife, and you
knew I loved him all the time—you devil!"

CHAPTER VII.

WANDERINGS.

" Such groans of roaring wind and rain, I never
Remember to have heard.....................
.....................The tempest in my mind
Doth from my senses take all feeling else,
Save what beats there."

SHAKSPERE (*King Lear*).

FOR the moment Leo did not realize the full significance of the destruction of his fondest hopes. Anger and contempt made the pain less keen, but when the door closed after him, shutting him out into the darkness and storm, a feeling of despairing helplessness took possession of him. He was cast forth from what he had always considered his home : she whom he had firmly believed in had destroyed his faith ; his love was hopeless; its object a shattered idol, forever beyond his reach. Where was he to go, to whom should he turn for sympathy and comfort ? If Rose was false,—Rose, in whom he had so faithfully, so unreservedly believed, could he trust any one ?

Hardly knowing what he did he tramped on through the rain, heedless of the mud in his path or where he was going. He saw a brilliantly-lighted liquor saloon and paused irresolutely to look in at the crowd of men who were drinking, smoking, and laughing before the bar. He was tempted to enter, but while he hesitated an intoxicated man stumbled forth, and he withdrew in disgust. "It has not come to that yet," he muttered as he resumed his walk. At length he began to feel tired and paused to look about him. He was upon the Cambridge Street drawbridge ; how he came there he had no idea. The rain was drizzling lazily, with a penetrating dampness, and a disagreeable

chill rose from the waters of the river. Up
and down the streets stretched long lines of
lights that were mirrored in the puddles and
reflected with a blurred faintness by the wet
pavements. The gas-jets burned with a
sickly yellow flame, made more ghastly by
the white, glaring electric lights. The
waters of the river, on either hand, were
masses of liquid blackness relieved by flash-
ing, zigzagging gleams, reflected from the
lights on the opposite shores. Leo peered
into the black waters but could see nothing.
" Black as death ! " he muttered. He heard
the lapping of the waves, and there seemed
to be a comforting message in the sound.
He peered guiltily about to see if he was
observed, and heard the click of horses' shoes
upon the pavement and the tinkling of a
bell as a horse-car approached. The clink-
ing changed to a thumping sound as the
horses stepped upon the bridge and Leo turned
slowly away from the water. His teeth

were chattering and he instinctively drew his coat tighter about him, muttering : "It's cold." Then, moved by a sudden impulse, he sprang upon the horse-car and rode into town.

At Bowdoin Square he left the car and resumed his weary tramp ; walking towards the heart of the city. A ragged little urchin followed him whining, "Please buy a paper, mister ! "

Leo stopped and looked sharply at the lad. "Why are you not at home ?" he asked gruffly, but not unkindly.

"I'm stuck on de papers," answered the lad, holding out a bundle of wet papers to prove his assertion.

" And if you sell them you'll go home ? "

" You bet ! "

" Here, give them to me," and Leo tossed the papers into the gutter and gave the boy a dollar. " Now go home," and without waiting for the urchin's thanks he walked on. "Even that shivering, poverty-stricken, little brat has a home," he thought bitterly, "I am more miserable than he." He turned to look back at the boy and saw he had gathered up the papers and was offering them to another passer. He laughed harshly. He passed along Tremont Row to Tremont Street, and noticed that they were usually crowded. The performance was over and the audience from the Museum was dispersing. He crossed the street to the new door of the theatre, and watched the people as they emerged. "What merry, bright faces, all happy and—" he thought with a sudden fury, "all false, false as Hell. Their smiles are lies, and I—I will lie too." He uttered a strange hoarse laugh that caused a timid little woman who was passing, to start and gaze into his face in alarm. The flushed features and wild eyes of the mud-bespattered man did not reassure her, and she clung closer to the arm of her escort.

A lady came from the theatre alone, and hurried to a carriage that was evidently awaiting her. As she entered the vehicle she glanced backward, and then, with a start of surprise, cried, "Leo!"

He started at the sound of his name and instinctively touched his hat. Advancing to see who it was that called, he grasped her proffered hand and cried, "You, Tiger Lily!"

"Miss Larry," she corrected him, smilingly.

"I believe *you* are my friend ; you said you were," he observed apathetically.

"Why, Leo, what ails you? You are soaking wet ; you look so strangely ; has anything happened? Jump into the carriage and tell me all about it."

Wearily Leo entered the carriage and sank down upon the cushioned seat with a sigh.

"Where to, miss?" asked the driver.

"Home, drive slowly."

"Now, Leo," she said, as the carriage moved along, "tell me all about it."

"There is nothing to tell," he answered. "Rose is married, that is all," and he laughed.

"Poor boy, poor boy!" she murmured sympathetically. "I can understand now."

"Never mind me," he said, attempting to rally himself. "How came you in Boston to-night?"

"We are laying over here until the first of the week, when we start on the circuit. You are wet through, surely you ought to take care of yourself."

"I don't care what becomes of me now," he cried wildly. "My life is a wreck. Do you know, I came near making an end of it all, to-night."

"Leo!"

"Yes, in my place some men would have killed themselves, but I—I did more; I lived."

" Poor boy, time will cure you, but it is hard. She must be heartless."

"I don't know ; she's false, though. I trusted her against the world, but it seems that she could not trust me against the first calumny that arose in my absence, she did not even try to hear my vindication. Well, I shall never believe again in friendship, in honesty, in—in love."

The carriage stopped. " Here I am," said Tiger Lily, preparing to alight. " What is your address ? I will tell the driver to take you home."

Leo sprang from the carriage. " Home !" he echoed, "I have none. I lived in the house with—her ; but now—well, I can take care of myself."

" Why, where are you going ? what will you do ? "

" I must write something for the paper to-night. I'll find some place to write in. I can't sleep."

"Look here, Leo, I'm not going to allow you to wander about on a night like this in the state of mind you are in ; it would be the death of you. Come into my parlor and write if you will, and perhaps Mrs. West can find a room for you."

"Well," said Leo, apathetically.

She opened the door with a latch-key and he followed her in. The hackman chuckled maliciously as they disappeared, and, whipping up his horses, drove from the street.

The next day Lester Ingraham called at a quiet boarding-house on Bulfinch Street, in answer to an urgent note, and was met by Tiger Lily.

"You are his friend," she said, "and I did not know who else to send for. Just look at him, poor boy."

Leo was lying upon a lounge in her private parlor, asleep. His face was flushed and his garments disordered. Every now and then he would move uneasily and mutter some incoherent words.

"How long has he been so?" asked Less.

She hesitated, and blushed hotly. "He—he came here last night and wrote for his paper. He had been wandering about the streets and was wet through. I left him after a while, and when I came back he was sleeping there. I could not disturb him, and so I—I allowed him to remain. He slept there all night in his damp clothes, and this morning I found him this way."

"We must remove him, Tiger Lily," said Less, gravely.

"Not for me, Less. If he is going to be ill he shall stay, and I will do what I can for him. Oh, they have acted shamefully to him! That woman, who would think it a disgrace to associate with me, has treated him as I would not treat a dog," she said, passionately.

"Rose Maynard? Yes, I have heard; it's

a very strange affair. We must have a doctor for him."

"Will you call one, please ? "

" Yes, I'll get Farnsworth, and I'll take his papers down to the *Hermes* office. A parable, I suppose."

"He said so. Oh, Less," she cried, with uncontrollable anxiety, "hurry for the doctor."

" Tiger Lily," said Less, gravely, "has our Scribe become so much to you ? "

"Yes, Less. Now go ! "

In the next number of *Hermes* this strange contribution from The Scribe appeared :

A FRAGMENT.

"My uneasiness had disappeared, and now all about me seemed vagueness, and in my mind, indifference. Another had sinned, and Justice, the blind goddess, seized upon me to expiate the crime. The hour of my doom was close at hand, yet I

9

recked little. They came, and I was led to the
verge of the hoary verdure-crowned cliff, rising
sheer from the lake in the valley. About me were
stern unpitying faces, but I sought no pity. I
thought not of what was to come, but only of the
beauty of nature as it lay in untrammeled grandeur
at my feet. Gentle breezes fanned my cheek and
whispered of courage, but I heeded not, I feared
not. The setting sun cast long rays from the
topmost peak of the distant mountains, over the
valley, silvering the waters of the lake with myr-
iads of sparkles, that grew paler and paler as
the great orb slowly sank behind the snow-clad
summits. Then, through the transparent waters,
methought I saw the gleaming domes and spires
of marble palaces, while faint sweet strains of
music—music of an unearthly sweetness—fell
upon my ears, but behind me boomed the harsh
clang of the great bell, sounding my knell and
drowning the strains.

" I was hurled from the dizzy height of the
cliff into the lake below. Down, down, down I
fell, the air rushing madly by me and the awful
whirl making my senses reel. I heard them
shout in triumph as I fell, they who had called
themselves my friends, and I was glad that I

was leaving forever their world, where deceit is king. Then I reached the water and the delicious coolness closed over me. I yielded to the pleasure of the change and sank, without a struggle. The last sun ray shot through the water beside me, lighting up my surroundings. I thought I saw shadowy forms, of beautiful mermaidens floating towards me, with outstretched arms and kindly, smiling faces. I longed for friendship; all I had left behind me were false; could these be true? I would have trusted them, I think, but ere they reached my side my senses fled."

PART II.

THE SPOT UPON THE TIGER LILY.

"My good stars that were my former guides
  Have empty left their orbs and shot their fires
  Into the abysm of Hell."

SHAKSPERE (*Antony and Cleopatra*).

CHAPTER I.

BOHEMIA.

"THE land of staunch comradeship, of kindly sympathy
......where the primitive virtues have fled for refuge
from the shams of society and where Mrs. Grundy holds no
sway."

HARRY HAMILTON.

MONTHS passed and the sweet softness of spring came again. It was at first rumored that Leo had suddenly disappeared and then, that he was ill. As he became convalescent and was seen, now and then, walking feebly about the quieter streets, people whispered, with knowing nods and smiles, that he had been lying at a boarding house where a noted burlesque actress, who had nursed him devotedly through his illness, and who compelled her manager to find a substitute for her during that time, made her home. No pains were taken to deny the story, and it was forgotten as soon as a new scandal arose. Every man of prominence, no matter how petty his prominence may be, will surely have some stories circulated about him relating to the low standard of his morals, and these stories are so often without foundation that it is difficult to distinguish the real sinners. Appreciating this fact Leo did not commit himself. Only a few of his nearest friends knew just how matters stood with him. When his strength was sufficiently restored he left Boston and was lost sight of by all in the city except Less, who knew he was following Durrell's company as a sort of hanger-on and who joined him whenever he could manufacture an excuse for so doing. Leo's studio remained closed all winter and the only indication that his acquaintances had of his being alive was the regular appearance of his parables in *Hermes.*

And all this time Rose lived in a magnificent home, provided with every comfort and luxury that money could procure. By every means in his power, Oliver Choate strove to make her happy, prompted to do so more because of the reproaches of his guilty conscience than anything else, but all his efforts were vain. She was like a wild bird, restlessly beating its wings against the bars of a gilded cage, vainly striving for the freedom it could not gain, and heedless of the glitter which surrounded it.

They never spoke of Leo, avoiding the subject by a sort of tacit understanding; Choate, because he feared the effect of mentioning her unforgotten lover to his wife, and Rose, because she did not wish to rouse her husband into speaking ill of one who was enshrined in her heart by a love crushed, but still alive. She did not credit the accusation Choate had made against Leo, and felt an antagonism against her husband

that she did not scruple to let him see. That he
could not hope for her love, Choate had known
from the first, but he had felt sure of retaining
her respect. Even that he was not destined
to have. Coldness and ofttimes .sneers were
the only thanks he received for his ..tten-
tions, and in many ways she made it obvious
to him that he was distasteful to her, that
she preferred other companionship to his,
until, at length, he went his way and she
hers, hardly seeing each other from one
week to another, and then meeting only
long enough to exchange a cold greeting.
This pleased Rose, because it left her free
to brood over her troubles and her fancied
wrongs. As for Choate, he cared not—his
love had always been, at best, but the piti-
ful, disgusting passion of an almost decrepit
man, and it had died forever, before Rose
was his, killed by the pangs of conscience that
tormented him ceaselessly from the moment
of Mrs. Maynard's death. He felt himself a

murderer : do what he might, the white face
of the dead woman, that ghastly nuptial
scene, haunted him always. His words had
killed her, she died from his lie, and she died
while he was still acting a lie to her. The
realization of this fact was slowly wearing
away his very life. He was glad of his es-
trangement from Rose, since the sight of her
called up visions of the dead ; she was the
fruit for which he had bartered his all, only
to find bitterness where he sought luscious
ripeness. Daily he seemed to grow more
feeble, and oftener and oftener he was dis-
turbed by visions of the dead that woke him
from his troubled sleep to torment him.
" Murderer ! " the pale lips seemed to whisper,
and he did not dare to pray ; he knew too
well that a fellow-being had died before her
time because of his lust.

Rose eagerly devoured the Scribe's corner
in *Hermes* every week and took advantage
of every means to learn any news, however

meagre, of Leo. The stories that were circulated reached her ears but did not serve to diminish her ever-increasing infatuation. She heard nothing direct from him nor did she know where he was. Once she met Less upon the street, and he bowed distantly. She was tempted to stop him and ask for news of Leo, but pride made her hesitate, and before she decided to speak he was gone. When she reached home she was glad that she had not spoken, but the incident so affected her that she shut herself into her room, and wept. Several times thereafter she thought of applying to Less for news of Leo, but always controlled the desire. Thus the time passed in the Choate household with both master and mistress miserably unhappy.

One day Less passed the familiar door in the long hall of "Bohemia," that delightful building under the roof of which are gathered the jolliest crowd of good fellows one can well think of; nearly all artists, their studios ranged side by side; Less passed the familiar door upon which was painted, "L. Ormsby, 81," and noticed · it was open. Uttering a shout of glad surprise he rushed in, without pausing to knock, and was warmly greeted by Leo and Durrell,

"Well, well," he cried, gazing from one to the other with unfeigned delight, "it does a fellow's heart good to see you again. Where did you spring from?"

"Seek not to know too much," answered Leo smilingly, "let it suffice that we have come. How are you?"

"I'm salubrious, but you're not looking well, Leo."

"Oh, I'm all right. It's my hair I suppose that changes me. That d——d fever last winter left me a goodly number of gray hairs as a remembrancer," and he coughed dryly.

"The truth of it all is," said Durrell, " that Leo won't take care of himself. We cannot influence him at all ; he simply goes it, all the time."

"That won't do, Leo——" began Less.

" Oh, dry up," said the object of their sympathy, impatiently, " I'm all right. Sit down if you can find a clean spot; such a dust I never saw. Say, Less, I've finished Diana."

" So I heard. Exhibited in New York. Who sat for it ?"

"Who do you suppose ?" laughed Durrell.

" Larry, of course," said Leo, "I had a good offer for it from the Hoffman House people but I won't sell my picture to a bar-room art-gallery, especially one in which she figures. I imagine they want it because the subject shows half nude women ; but as for hanging my work up as that Bogoreau is hung, for half drunken men to leer and gloat over—— Bah! You both know what Larry and I are to each other, but I want it understood that I respect her above any other woman alive to-day, and that's why I refused the biggest offer I ever had for a work of mine, and I'm not sorry for it."

" I can appreciate your motives, Leo," said Less, "but you go a bit farther than I would."

" I suppose you think me an odd stick," replied Leo, " and sometimes I am unable to understand myself. There is a difference in my regard for Larry, I fear, from what I used to feel for others. I remember how uncomfortable I used to feel when I found myself in company with one of those men who are given to making questionable remarks and telling *risque* stories before ladies. There is no resenting the remarks of such fellows, they are too guarded for that. I was inexperienced then," he continued, with a hard laugh, "and thought of my lady friends with a sort of reverence and such remarks seemed to me as blasphemy does to a priest. Perhaps the purity of woman was a part of my religion, and evidence that she has vulgar traits in common with man hurt me because it tended to destroy the ideal I had formed of that which I have since learned does not exist—a perfect woman."

"No," said Less philosophically. "A fellow should never marry, because if he gets a homely girl, she will be too disagreeable an object for him to gaze upon day after day, and if she's handsome she'll be too agreeable an object for other fellows to gaze upon. Either way is wrong ; best to remain a jolly bachelor, like me."

"There is such a thing as drawing a prize."

"Why not trust to Providence and run your chances ?" laughingly suggested Durrell.

" Providence, eh ? Say, Durrell, are you religious ? "

" I suppose so."

" That's a pretty weak answer. I'm not. You just take your prayer-book in one hand and your pocket-book in the other and see which will go farthest in this world."

" How about the next ? " suggested Less.

" Let us have less of the threat of Hell in the hereafter and a little more of it here."

" What do you mean ? "

" Hell is the terror that holds in check the evil tendencies of man. Let the laws of our land be annulled for a day, can you imagine what excesses would result ? That's what I mean ; but dropping religion, what brings you back ? "

" King Robert of Sicily," replied Leo, with a dramatic wave of his arm.

" Oh, get out ! Be serious."

" I am. My play is to be produced at the Boston, in a fortnight."

10

" You don't say so ? "

" Yes, I do."

" It's a great piece," said Durrell, "and ought to go, but wait until you see the new one he is doing for me."

" What's the subject ? "

" The Diver," said Leo good-naturedly, " after Schiller—a long way."

" You'll hardly recognize King Robert now," said Durrell, " since it has been re-written."

" Tiger Lily takes the leading part of course ? "

" Of course, and she'll make a queenly king."

Leo began laughing, but was suddenly attacked with a severe coughing spell. Less regarded his friend anxiously. " Look here, old man," he said solicitously, " you ought to do something for that cough."

" Oh, Larry is dosing me all the time," he returned lightly.

" But you should see a doctor."

" Bah ! I'm not sick, and I won't have a lot of nasty medicines poured into me. I'll be all right in a little while. It's only an obstinate cold."

" I should say it was obstinate," said Durrell, " he's been coughing all winter."

" Oh, drop it," cried Leo impatiently.

" Where's Tiger Lily ?" asked Less.

" She's at Mrs. West's with Ada."

" With Ada ?"

" Yes. Guida has an engagement with another company and we are looking after the child ; in fact, between ourselves, we have adopted her."

" It's a good job for the chicken that she is under the maternal wing, or I should say petal, of Tiger Lily. Guida is not a model mother," observed Durrell.

" What can you expect ?" said Less, with a shrug of his shoulders. " A lively actress can't make a good mother."

" I don't know about that" cried Leo,
" look at Larry."

" Is she a mother ? "

" To Ada, yes, and a good one."

" And Leo plays papa to perfection,"
laughed Durrell.

" By Jove, Less, no man can have a better
friend than I have in Larry," cried Leo, im-
pulsively, "I know the world sneers and
looks upon our relations as wrong, let them
if they will, but in my presence no one shall
speak disparagingly of her. She has every
quality that goes to make up a good woman
and she is a good woman. There are women
to-day who have lied, cheated, blasphemed,
broken their parents' hearts, in fact, violated
nearly every one of God's commandments,
yet society overlooks their shortcomings and
welcomes them with open arms. There are
others, like my poor Larry, who are innocent
of all these sins, but who have disregarded
the seventh commandment, and these are

outcasts, beyond redemption. To them the doors of society are forever closed, they are beyond hope of forgiveness. No matter how bitter their tears, no matter how repentant they are, they will be thrust forth, back to their sin, to sink deeper and deeper until they are utterly lost, when a kindly word and a helping hand would be their salvation. They are branded with a mark worse than a felon's and more indelible, by those who, perhaps, are far greater sinners. And this is Justice, this is Society. Bah !"

"Write that in a parable," said Less, seriously.

" Perhaps I will."

" What did you write last week ?" asked Durrell, "I did not see it."

" Here it is," said Leo, tossing him a copy of *Hermes.*

" Read it aloud, Durrell," cried Less.

And Durrell read :—

"'Once there lived a very learned man. From dawn till midnight he pored over his studies, tirelessly seeking to increase his knowledge. "Knowledge is power," he said, "and I would know all, to be all-powerful." Every pleasure, even social intercourse with his fellows he denied himself, in his lust for learning. "I know more than they," he thought, "they can teach me naught, therefore I'll none of their company." He saw a beautiful maiden and his heart beat faster in her presence, and he desired her. She smiled upon him and modestly showed her preference for him, but just then happened strange things among the stars; and while he studied the heavenly bodies he forgot earth, himself, and the maid, and she passed from his life. Thus in loneliness and study, casting aside all the joys of life did he pass his days until his time was come and he died.

"' Before the great judgment-seat he came and the recording angel asked of him, "Who art thou?"

"'"I am he that was most learned," he made reply.

"'Then was judgment passed upon him. "Earth was made for man and filled with all that

is best for his good. For learning, you cast aside
everything, held yourself above your fellow-men
and aspired to the forbidden. You refused the
good it pleased the Lord to provide for you on
earth, therefore you are unfit for the joys of
Heaven. Go, sit without and take such joy from
thy learning as it will yield. Here is no place
for thee.'"

"Say, Leo what made you strike that
religious vein?"

"There's very little religion in that," was
the reply. "There are any number of as-
pects to look at the question touched upon
in that parable form. The next number will
give another point of view of the same
thing. Here are the proofs."

"May we see?"

"Certainly."

Less took the proof-sheets and read aloud:—

"'A child lived in the most squalid quarter of
a densely populated city. Ill-treatment, misery,
and starvation were his lot, but still he thrived.

Ignorance and neglect were his tutors, and when he saw the splendor of the rich, he said, " I would fain live thus," nor was it envy that prompted the thought, but a desire for the good things nature provides for man. And as he grew to manhood the desire became stronger in him, but strive as he would to rise, his ignorance always held him back. He saw a fair woman and he desired her for his own with a pure passion, but a rich man came and the woman laughed and followed him. Then he grew desperate and brooded. Why should he live always in misery while others were happy and in the possession of plenty? His discontent made him ill, and he wandered feebly about the streets penniless, and hunger attacked him, so he stole, but the officers of Justice seized him and cast him into prison, and there he died.

"'And conscious of his shortcomings he came before the great Throne of God.

"'"Who art thou?" he was asked.

"'"1 am a felon," he replied, and fell upon his face.

"'And the great book of life was opened to where his story was writ, and reading it, the Almighty spake, saying, "Lo! this man's sin hath been atoned by the woe it hath worked upon his soul. He hath not had his share of what was created for man's enjoyment, therefore shall he taste the joys of after-life. Let him enter the Kingdom of Heaven.'"

"I suppose there's no religion in that either, Leo, eh?" queried Less, maliciously.

"Less, perhaps, than you think," was the reply, "outside of the form. You know religion is a subject that does not trouble me much."

"I've never heard your religious views," said Durrell.

"They are simple," replied Leo. "'Love thy neighbor as thyself,' is all the religion I require. I find it hard to live up to that precept and until I can do so it would be nonsense to profess anything further."

"But you believe in a God?"

"No one can tell me more than I already know and that is—nothing. I do not deny that there is a God. I do not know. What I do know, and feel, and worship, is the loveliness of nature ; and, if there is a God, in enjoying His works I feel that I am praising Him, and that I am doing my duty as a man."

They were interrupted by a rap at the door and a newsboy entered.

"Saw you was back, Mr. Ormsby, an' thought you might want papers again, sir," he said, with a grin.

"All right, Tim," said Leo, "leave them as usual."

"Thank'ee, sir," said the boy, laying some papers on the table and going out.

"Any news ?" asked Less, lazily, as he lighted a cigarette.

"Don't see anything," replied Leo, glancing rapidly through the columns.

"No," added Durrell, who had picked up one of the papers, "not a word about the company either. Hullo! Leo, isn't this a friend of yours ? I think I've heard you mention the name, Oliver Choate ?"

"What is it?" asked Leo, in a strained tone.

"Dead," laconically replied Durrell.

Leo snatched the paper from his hands and looked for himself. Yes, there it was in black and white.

> "**Choate, Oliver.** Age 63, in this city, April 21st; funeral Tuesday at 11 A. M. from residence, —— Commonwealth Avenue."

Leo tossed the paper aside thoughtfully and sank heavily into a chair. His face was very pale, and Less regarded him anxiously for a moment but, seeing that he was quite self-possessed, he turned to Durrell saying,

"We'd better be going now, Charlie."

"Come on then. See you later, Leo," and the two men went out.

"You put your foot into it that time, Durrell," said Less, when they were alone.

"Well, I didn't know," he replied, "I

wouldn't have wounded Leo for the world. Who the devil's Choate?"

"He's the old duffer who married Rose, Leo's girl, you know."

Durrell gave a long whistle. "And she's a widow now, rich too, I suppose."

"Yes."

"And the coast's clear for Leo."

"As far as I know. There's Tiger Lily though."

"She don't count ; girls of that kind never do in such cases. Leo 'll drop her I suppose."

"I suppose so. Poor girl, and she's so devoted to him."

CHAPTER II.

" Lo, where the stage—the poor, degraded stage—
Holds its warped mirror to a gaping age."
CHARLES SPRAGUE.

ACTIVE preparations were in progress for the production of Leo's play. The dead walls throughout the city were covered with glaring lithographs and little skits appeared daily in the papers, telling an expectant public of new glories, designed by the lavish management to please their patrons. Leo had been compelled to so re-write the play, that it bore but little resemblance to what it was originally intended to be. An Amazon march, a ballet festival, and numerous songs and dances had been introduced, giving scope for glittering spectacular effects but necessitating a merciless cutting and maiming of the dialogue; and even such parts as were left intact, the players distorted whenever there was an opportunity of introducing some puerile joke. There had originally been a Gilbertian quality to the lines, but the changes blunted their point. Still, Durrell and his stage manager were confident that the piece would make an instantaneous success, and although Leo was annoyed at the mutilation of his work he permitted it in deference to the experience and superior judgment of the others. Every day there were rehearsals at which Durrell, his stage-manager and Leo in turn, stormed and swore at the stupidity of stage-hands and chorus-girls. It was an uninterrupted grind, drill, drill, drill, until an idea of what was expected of them began to pierce their density and the prospect of a good first performance brightened. Tiger Lily was indefatigable in her efforts to assure the success of the play, and managed to instil some of her enthusiasm into the other members of the cast. Little Ada was her especial pupil, and was charming as a cherub, acting and singing with an intelligence and precision remarkable in a child. " I must do my very best," she said, " 'cause this is Leo's play."

At length the eventful Monday arrived. The day before a full-dress rehearsal had been held, and all that day the weaker members of the cast were drilled. Leo was dressed at an early hour and, after a hasty bite at Clark's, turned down Mason Street to the dingy stage-entrance of the theatre and bestowing a cigar upon Con, the doorkeeper, as he passed, went upon the stage. It was early and but few of the company were about. The stage manager was busy giving some final directions to the stage carpenters, and in superintending the setting of the scenery for the first act; a grand cathedral interior which changed to the palace of King Robert. The gas-men were laying hose for their lights and in one corner were testing a sort of a magic-lantern, which reflected swiftly moving clouds upon the scene. The lights were very dim, and sound of hammers now and again heard, as the carpenters fastened some piece of scenery into place, echoed hollowly through the vast barn-like building. The curtain was up and a fluttering of ghostly white draperies was visible in the auditorium, as the attendants removed the cloths that covered the gilding and draperies in the house, and protected them from dust, during the day.

"What's the time, Mr. Ormsby?" asked the stage manager.

"Ten minutes past seven."

"Say," he shouted to some one in the body of the house, "what time do you open the doors here?"

"Seven fifteen."

"Time to light up," he said, turning to the gas-man.

" All right.   Hillo, Bill—Bill ! "

A voice from above replied, " Hullo ! "

"Ring down the- curtain."

The gas-man went to a spot at the right of the proscenium, where a number of wheels projected from a marble slab set in the wall; he turned some of these and with a sudden flash, the lights in the auditorium burned up.   There was a grating sound and the green curtain descended shutting the house from sight.

The company was beginning to assemble, chattering and laughing as they came upon the stage, or made their way to the dressing-rooms.   Suddenly there was a loud trampling rush heard together with the hum of many voices.   "There goes the gallery," said a stage hand, "the doors are open."

Leo had come early, thinking he might be of some use, but found nothing to do, and

11

stood idly looking at the contrivances about him, so simple, and yet, to the uninitiated, apparently complicated. He was full of excitement but outwardly calm, save that his face was flushed and his cough troubled him unusually.

"Well, Leo, will I do?" asked a pleasant voice at his side, and turning, he beheld a kingly figure clad in royal purple with crown and sceptre complete. The king's robe was open, however, and showed, beneath, the motley garb of a jester with the cap and bauble thrust into the belt for convenience.

"Charming, Larry," he replied with a smile. "Ah, here's Ada."

"Hullo, Leo," cried the child, running to him, "I haven't seen you all day. Isn't my costume nice?"

"Very nice, little one."

"But, Leo, I s'posed angels had big wings and long white robes. You see they've made me different."

"Well, you're a cherub, you see," he replied, "the cherub does the acting in this play and the others are only in the transformation.".

"They're only supers?"

"That's all."

"And I'm an actress?"

"And a charming little one, at that," assented Leo, taking the child in his arms.

"Now I want you to wish me luck in my new part."

"I do."

"And Tiger Lily?"

"And Tiger Lily too."

"And we both wish you luck in your new play, don't we, Tiger Lily?"

"Indeed we do, Cherub, and if it depends upon us——"

"It'll be a go," said the child, finishing the sentence.

The people who were to appear in the play were flocking upon the stage, a motley assemblage of courtiers, ladies, soldiers, sailors, priests, nuns, peasants and ballet-dancers, and a perfect babel of subdued voices sounded through the place.

"Say, Leo," said Ada, with an air of professional concern, " How's the house ? "

" I haven't looked, little one."

" Let me peep, will you ? " she whispered eagerly.

Leo led the child to the side of the proscenium where, through a small opening, the front of the theatre was visible.

" O-o-o-o-h ! " cried Ada, as she looked through, " It's packed, and there's Less in the box ; look, Leo."

Leo obediently applied his eye to the " peep-hole " and saw a vast, indistinct sea of faces filling the building from floor to ceiling. He glanced at the opposite box and there, sure enough, sat Less. Mechanically he nodded and smiled at his friend, whereat little Ada laughed heartily, and, joining in her mirth, he stepped aside to allow Tiger Lily to look.

The sharp burr of an electric bell echoed through the theatre and a call for the orchestra was heard. The gas engineer turned a few of the many stop-cocks upon the wall by the prompter's desk and the lights in the front of the house flashed out in full brilliancy.

"There's the call!" said Tiger Lily, as she fastened King Robert's robe, hiding the jester's dress beneath.

The first strains of the overture became audible, long, low chords, swelling into an impressive anthem, making the call-boy's summons, "All on for the first act," inaudible to the audience.

"Come Ada, we must go," said Tiger Lily.

"Good luck go with you," said Leo, with a smile.

"Amen, to that, dear," replied Tiger

Lily, " since luck to me to-night is luck for you."

Left alone, Leo felt nervous for the first time. His heart beat rapidly and he felt a sense of suffocation. Shaking himself impatiently he coughed and turned to examine the stage. Everything was in readiness for the rising of the curtain. The altar of the mimic church was aglow with candles, the altar boys stood in their places, while the stage manager and his assistants, in their shirt-sleeves—inharmonious fellows—were lighting incense in the chalices. The congregation was in place, but as yet wore anything but a devout look ; and over, opposite, upon a raised dais, surrounded by sparsely clad pages whose sex was very apparent, sat King Robert, who, as Leo glanced that way, smiled and nodded. The overture ended with a crash ; there was an expectant stir in the audience ; the stage manager took one last hurried survey of his work,

cried, "All ready!" and stepped out of
sight; the gas-man turned on his stage-
lights and darkened the front of the house ;
the company took their positions; the
prompter signalled the musical director;
the music began ; the chorus raised their
voices in a solemn anthem ; the curtain rose,
and the play began.

The church effect was a good one and im-
pressed the audience, a fact which the per-
formers were not slow to realize, and feeling that their efforts were meeting with ap-
proval, they entered into the spirit of their
respective parts with renewed interest. The
church services end after King Robert's scorn-
ful defiance of the heavenly powers and the
altar-lights are quenched. Gradually the
church becomes deserted until the king,
asleep in his chair of state, is left alone
attended only by his pages. The lads dare
not wake him, and at first regard their position as great fun, laughing, joking and

singing among themselves, but night is
falling, the gloomy old cathedral grows
dark and darker, until no light is seen save
where the faint rays of the rising moon
filter through the stained glass windows.
The boys grow timorous, still the king
sleeps, and his pages determine to find a
light. They grope about, starting away
now and then, from dark corners where the
shadows seem to move, or from the ghostly
figure of some marble saint, looming white
and threatening out of the darkness. One
lad bumps into another and both cry out in
terror, frightening their comrades still more,
and an ominous thunderclap in the apparently clear sky completes their panic. They
rush from the place, closing the door, in
which there is a spring-lock, behind them,
and the king is alone, locked in the church.
The light streaming through the great
stained glass windows increases in brilliancy
until it seems that there is nothing between

it and the beholder. A cloud floats to the window and reclining upon it lies a dimpled cherub—Ada. Then King Robert wakes to find himself a jester. The cherub tells him his doom ; he laughs, defies, and finally growing enraged, rushes up the altar at the cherub, but the visitor is gone and blackness reigns again. His rage bursts forth anew. God, man or devil shall not stop him, and mounting the altar, he dashes a heavy candelabrum through the painted window and climbs out into the night while thunder booms overhead and sharp lightning luridly illumines the scene.

The audience received this scene with generous applause, and a feeling that the play was a success began to manifest itself in the minds of those behind the scenes. In the darkness following King Robert's exit the scene was rapidly changed to his palace, and when the lights were turned up the sudden change from the gloomy church to the brilliant palace drew forth another burst of applause. King Robert returns to find himself, in truth, a jester, and another ruling in his palace, and the act ends with his despairing realization of his helplessness.

The curtain had hardly fallen before there was a general rush and scramble, apparently in aimless confusion, but in reality quite methodical. The gorgeous palace was dismantled with surprising rapidity and a lovely Sicilian landscape replaced it. Ada, having no change of costume to make, stood in the wings with Leo, during the wait, chattering merrily.

The second act shows the angel king's departure upon a pilgrimage to Rome, and the festivities attending it, and principally consists of dancing and marches. The final incident is the re-appearance of the cherub to King Robert to ask, "Who art thou?" and ·receive the proud reply, "I am the king!" At which, with a sorrowful smile

she points to the magnificent galley in which
are gathered the angel king and his following, and disappears. A crowd of jeering
peasants seize upon King Robert, seat him
backward upon an ass, and drive him upon
the galley, which sails away amid cheers and
laughter. In the third and last act King
Robert realizes the meaning of his punishment, and when asked again by the cherub,
"Who art thou?" replies humbly, "Thou
knowest best." Upon which his rightful place
is restored to him, and the play ends with a
gorgeous transformation, showing the cherub
ascending through tier on tier of clouds, by
other cherubs and angels in picturesque atti-
tudes, to a golden gate, from which streams
a dazzling light.

The audience was demonstrative, and there
was a recall after each act. At the end, in
answer to a storm of applause, the curtain
was again raised and Tiger Lily and Ada
stepped forward bowing, for upon them the

evening's chief success had fallen. Tiger Lily whispered something to Ada, and the child, comprehending instantly, darted to the wings where Leo was standing, and seizing one of his hands in both of hers, pulled lustily. So unexpected was this action that, before he was quite aware of its drift, Leo was in the glare of the footlights, looking through the tremulous curtain of heat that rose from them, at the noisy multitude in front, and bowing his thanks. The curtain fell again and the stage hands began to clear up, preparatory to going home. In a few moments the curtain was again raised, disclosing the deserted theatre in darkness once more, and the company began leaving, one by one. What had a few moments before been brilliant with light and beauty was now a vast dark place, smelling of burned gas, the gloom broken only here and there by the light of a sickly wire-covered gas jet.

'Well it's a go, Leo, my boy," cried Durrell as he came upon the stage by the little private door, near the gas table.

" Do you think so ? "

" I know it ; look at the reception it had."

" The papers will tell to-morrow."

" Devil take the papers ! The piece will go no matter what they say. I'm so satisfied of that, that I'm going to book it for the whole of next season. There's a barrel of money in it."

" I am thinking of the literary rank it will take," said Leo.

" That's all bosh, Leo, don't bother your head about rank. Look at H—t, he has no literary rank, but he makes money. Take my advice and write a few things that will make money for your manager, and then you can get anything you please staged—otherwise no one will bother with you. You've got a start now, make the most of it."

"Thanks to you, old man, for that start," said Leo warmly, grasping Durrell's hand "but you don't understand my aims, I think."

" Perhaps not," returned Durrell with a shrug, " you poets are a queer lot, anyhow, and hanged if I believe you understand yourselves half the time."

" Are you coming with us, Leo ?" asked Tiger Lily, as she emerged from the dressing-rooms with Ada, clad for the street.

Leo coughed. " I think I will, Larry," he answered, " my cough is troublesome to-night and perhaps I'd better not hang around with the boys ; still, to-night is—" and he hesitated.

"Go on, Leo," urged Durrell, kindly, " you're not fit to knock about to-night. Go home and nurse yourself, and I'll see that they all drink to your success."

" All right, and say, Durrell, invite them to join me to-morrow night, after the show at Ober's for a little supper, will you ? Boys and girls both."

" I will."

" All right.   Good-night."

" Good-night."

The next morning Less called upon Leo at
an early hour to congratulate him upon the
successful production of his play.   He found
him with the morning papers scattered all
about him.   "Hullo!" he cried cheerily,
"looking up the criticisms? How are
they?"

"They all commend the scenery, the acting
and the production in general ; there is little
said about the play," was the bitter reply.

" Because it was a success, I suppose."

"Success! Why, anything put on with
the gorgeousness Durrell has mounted it
with, would succeed, but I had some idea
that my work was a little above the ordinary burlesque.   In fact, I know it was,
before they tampered with it, but—well, my

eyes are opened ; it is a failure as far as I am concerned."

"Oh, bosh !"

"Listen to this," and he read from one of the papers :—

"'The play is founded upon Longfellow's well-known "Tale of a Way-side Inn," and is a good vehicle for the display of the company's talents. It is after the style of all burlesques, perhaps better written than the average, with brilliant lines here and there, but there is nothing in it destined to outlive the local celebrity it may gain.'

"Does that sound like success ?"

"My dear boy," cried Less, "that is only the opinion of one young man."

"Here are half a dozen more to uphold his opinion," answered Leo, indicating the papers.

"Wait and see the crowded houses it will draw.   That is the true test."

"The crowd is attracted by the glitter and dancing, not by the literary merit of the play. Durrell might as well have a mess of 'rot' like 'Adonis'; it would draw as well."

"Oh, pshaw ! you are too nice altogether ; they don't find fault with your play," cried Less.

"There's a difference between fault-finding and criticism," replied Leo, "they simply pass over the play, as if it were too trivial to notice at length. Have you seen the morning *A——r* ? "

"No."

"Read it, there is the opinion of a man whose praise would, to me, outweigh the censure of every other critic in the city," and Leo handed him the paper. Less read rapidly :—

"The announcement of a play, or burlesque, from the pen of "The Scribe" of *Hermes*, drew us to the Boston Theatre in the expectation of a treat. We regret to chronicle our disappointment. The piece is called 'King Robert of Sicily,'

12

and follows closely the story of Longfellow's
poem. Had the writer omitted the burlesque
features of his work, it would have been far more
artistic. As it is, there are some parts worthy
of a word of praise, notably the first scene, but
as a whole, the action drags, being overburdened
with songs, dances, marches, and the usual in-
cidents of burlesque. There are many traces of
'cuts' in the dialogue, but whether these cuts
are made because of the dulness of the text or
to introduce 'specialties,' is hard to say. Altogether, the piece resembles what it was intended to be in about the degree that a tack-ham-
mer resembles a battle-axe. After he has given
us so many readable parables im *Hermes*, 'The
Scribe' should hesitate before presenting a work
so far below his proven ability."

"That's too bad," cried Less, dropping
the paper, "it's unjustly severe and charac-
teristic of C——'s criticisms."

"No, I think not," said Leo. "When
Durrell first proposed to produce the play, I
objected to the alterations and to making a
'leg show' of it. After my illness I didn't

care, and let them do as they pleased. The alterations may have secured the financial success of the work, but they denuded it of all literary value. I was conscious at first that this would be the case, but in the bustle of preparation I forgot—and now——"

"Never mind, Leo," said Less, encouragingly, "you can make it up on the new play."

" 'The Diver,' yes, it is nearly completed, and I will make it prove—what it will prove," and he laughed.

"We shall all look forward to it," cried Less, cheerfully, "and now I must be going."

"You'll join us at Ober's, to-night?"

"Oh, I'll be on hand, just say supper and I'm there ; but you ought to swear off, old man, until you get rid of that cough."

"I mean to. This is to be my last supper."

"Until you are better."

"Of course."

"Well, once more, good-morning."

"Good-morning."

CHAPTER III.

TWO WOMEN.

"Who hath not found himself surprised into revenge or action, or passion for good or evil, whereof the seeds lay within him, latent and unsuspected, until the occasion called them forth."

"THIS is Mr. Ormsby's settin'-room, Miss," said the maid at Mrs. West's as she ushered a heavily-veiled lady, attired in deep mourning, into Leo's study, "he'll be in soon."

"Very well, I will wait," replied the lady.

"Shall I tell Miss Varney you are here?"

"No!" cried the visitor, turning fiercely upon the girl. "I wish to see Mr. Ormsby alone," she continued in a gentler tone, "upon a private matter."

"Yes'm," said the girl, "I'll send him to

you as soon as he comes," and she quietly left the room.

The visitor looked curiously about, examining the contents of the room with much interest. Seating herself at a large writing-table she began turning over the confused heaps of manuscript lying thereon, now and then reading a few lines. A heavy sigh escaped her, and she murmured, "Parables and parables. Poor Leo, always recording his experiences thus. It brings him celebrity; the inestimable advantage of being known to those who do not know us," and she smiled faintly.

"Are you waiting for Leo?" suddenly asked a childish voice.

Rose started and turning, saw Ada standing by her side. "How you startled me, child," she exclaimed with a sigh. "Are you a fairy, that you come so noiselessly?"

"No, but Leo sometimes calls me cherub."

"Indeed, and who are you?"

" You mean really ? "

" Yes."

" I'm Ada, I'm the cherub in ' King Robert,' you know."

" Oh, you are the little child they speak of ? "

" Yes," replied Ada in a business-like tone. " I made a hit and got a lot of good notices in the papers."

" Come here and talk to me."

"I haven't much time," replied Ada, " Tiger Lily is waiting for me."

" And who is Tiger Lily ? "

"Why, aren't you acquainted with her ? She's our leading lady.   Leo calls her Larry."

" Oh, that woman ! " exclaimed Rose in a tone of contempt.

"Guess I can't stay, long's you speak of Tiger Lily like that," said Ada, promptly, and she marched towards the door with a dignified air.

" Oh, you mistake me," cried Rose hastily,

"I meant nothing. Do come and talk to me."

Ada turned and, after a careful scrutiny of Rose, observed gravely, "I haven't made up my mind whether I shall like you or not. Why don't you uncover your face?"

Rose smiled and raised her veil.

"Are you a friend of Leo's?" asked Ada.

"Yes, we are very old friends."

"What's your name?"

"Rose."

"I never heard him speak about you."

Rose winced. "We had a misunderstanding," she said.

"Oh, I see; and you came to make up."

Rose blushed, "To—to explain, perhaps."

"It's all the same."

"Is my catechism over?" asked Rose, with a feeling of angry amusement.

Ada ignored the question entirely; she was still studying Leo's visitor.

"You're in mourning," she observed.

"Yes, for my husband."

"Ah, I know now?" ejaculated Ada.

"What do you know!"

"Say, was your husband an old duffer?"

Rose started and eyed Ada intently, but perceiving that her strange question was asked seriously and in perfect innocence, and being anxious to learn what she could from the child she answered, "He was my senior. Why do you ask?"

"Then you're the one."

"What do you mean, child!"

"Less said a girl threw Leo over for an old duffer, and he's been a different fellow since. Your husband's dead, and now you want to make up with Leo, that's it!" cried Ada, triumphantly.

Rose blushed hotly. "Hush, child, hush, you should not speak of things of which you know nothing."

"But I do know," insisted the child. "You're so red it shows I do. It's no use,

though ; Less said you wasn't in it. Tiger
Lily stands first show, I heard him tell Durrell."

'You don't know what you are saying,
child," gasped Rose.

"Don't I, though ? Tiger Lily an' Leo 've
adopted me, and I ought to know."

"Are—are they married ?" queried Rose
anxiously.

"I don't know. If I did, I wouldn't tell.
I don't like you."

"Ada, Ada !" called a musical voice without, and in a moment the door opened and
Tiger Lily entered. "I beg your pardon,"
she said as she caught sight of Rose, "I did
not know that Mr. Ormsby had callers.
Come, Ada."

"She's waiting for Leo," said the child,
pointing to Rose.

"I am sorry Mr. Ormsby is not in," said
Tiger Lily, pleasantly. "Can I do anything
for you ?"

" Do you manage his affairs ? " asked Rose, with a sneer.

Tiger Lily blushed. "I often assist him with his writing," she answered.

" Tiger Lily," whispered Ada, audibly, tugging at her dress, "do you know her ? "

" No, dear."

" I do. She's the one who threw Leo over for the old duffer. She wants to make up."

The actress started and turned pale. Rose laughed unpleasantly. "My very original identification by that precocious child does not seem to please you," she observed.

" It startled me," admitted Tiger Lily, faintly.

" Will you permit me to ask a delicate question ? "

" What is it ? "

" Are you married ? "

" She asked me that," cried Ada, " and I wouldn't tell her."

Tiger Lily sank into a chair, and every vestige of color left her face.

Rose seemed to gloat over the suffering of her rival as she stood before her, smiling mockingly.

"Hush, Ada," whispered Tiger Lily, then, turning to Rose she said huskily, "I am not."

"I thought so."

"Why do you ask ?"

"Simply out of curiosity. I have heard that about you which makes me think you should be," replied Rose, insolently.

"Let me judge of that, if you please."

"Certainly, Miss—er—Tiger Lily."

"Miss Varney, if you please."

"Ah, yes, Varney. And Mr. Ormsby has been one of your followers since I saw him last, I suppose ? "

" On the night you told him of your marriage, I found him wandering about the streets, dazed by the shock of suddenly realizing your duplicity," said Tiger Lily rising from her chair with dignity ; she spoke hotly, but realizing that she was moved, controlled herself. "I nursed him through a terrible fever which left him a gray-haired wreck of his former self, and you, madam, are wholly and entirely to blame for it. You affect to sneer at me because I choose to live with him without our having been wedded, but you have no moral right to do so, for you sold yourself in marriage to an old man whom you could not love, while I give myself to the man I love, asking nothing in return."

" At least," sneered Rose, " I am an honest woman."

" Not at heart."

" What do you mean by that ? " asked Rose wrathfully.

" Ask yourself," quietly returned Tiger Lily.

" You are indulging this child in a rare treat by allowing her to hear this edifying conversation," said Rose, shifting to another point of attack in order to cover her weakness. "Is this your method of educating her ?"

"You began the conversation and for what she has heard you are to blame," retorted the actress, "Ada, please go up-stairs."

"All right," said the child, "but if you want me, just call," then, as she left the room, she pointed to Rose and cried vehemently, "I hate her."

"You will try to prevent my having an interview with Leo, I suppose ?" said Rose, defiantly.

"I shall do nothing of the kind," was the calmly spoken reply.

"Do not be too sure of your power over him."

"I am not."

"I mean to try to induce him to abandon the life he is leading," said Rose, trying to rouse her rival again.

"I shall be glad if you can do so."

"Then you are tired of him already !" cried Rose with a look of disgust.

"What a narrow mind you have !" exclaimed Tiger Lily, contemptuously, "I do not believe you are capable of feeling true love. You look at everything from a selfish standpoint. Can you not appreciate the fact that I wish you success because it is for his good ?"

"How noble !" sneered Rose. "Are there many women of your stamp who harbor such sentiments, or are you merely reciting for my benefit some of the mock heroics of the stage ?"

"I am learning to think less of you with every word you speak, and God knows my opinion was poor enough from the first," said Tiger Lily bitterly.

"Your opinion," echoed Rose scornfully ; "do you think I would turn my hand to alter in any way the opinion a shameless, abandoned woman might have of me ? "

"Rose!" exclaimed a familiar voice, sternly, as the door of the room opened, and Leo stood between the excited women.

"Leo!" cried Rose, taken aback by his sudden appearance, then, as she looked well at him, "Good Heavens! you are ill. Why —why Leo! your hair——"

"Do not trouble about my appearance, Mrs. Choate," said Leo coldly. "To what do I owe the honor of this visit?"

Rose controlled the alarm caused by the sudden and unexpected sight of his changed appearance, and with a sinking at heart, caused by his cold manner, replied, tremulously, "I came to see you—to explain, and this woman——"

"This lady is my best friend. I will not hear one word against her," he interrupted. "As for your explanation, it is unnecessary. I understand all the circumstances, and my sufferings are past, forgotten, and their cause forgiven."

Rose was taken aback ; this was hardly the reception she had looked for, and she felt at a loss for words to express herself fitly, still she blundered on, with a fierce determination to follow things to the end, but conscious that she was at a disadvantage. In an agitated voice she cried, " You are looking badly, Leo ; you are pale, ill. The life you are leading is killing you. I entreat you return to your old friends, your old life."

" My present friends satisfy me." .

" And they will kill you," she cried vehemently.

"My old friends have nearly done that," he retorted cuttingly.

" Leo, that is cruel," said Rose, with a little sob.

" We can both be cruel, Rose."

" Can my words have lost all weight with you ? " she murmured.

" All. You forfeited my esteem when you married. Larry here has it all now."

"And you dare to say that to me?" she cried angrily. "Do you know what people say of you."

"Disdain is the weapon with which to crush calumny," he answered calmly.

"Calumny?" repeated Rose, with ironical wonder.

"All scandal is calumny. It hears but one side."

"I do not wish to hear your excuses," said Rose, contemptuously.

"I have none to offer. I am no hypocrite, even though hypocrisy is a fashionable vice, and fashionable vices pass for virtues."

"You are not the Leo I once knew," said Rose, with a sorrowful shake of her head. "Had I thought of you like this I should not have come here. I will go."

"One moment," said Leo, "you asked me to return to my old friends, thus signifying your willingness to accept me as a friend again. Do you mean it?"

13

"Indeed I do," cried Rose eagerly.

"And will you also accept Larry as a friend?"

"No, never," she answered haughtily.

'Why not?"

"Can you ask why I will not accept an abandoned woman as a friend?"

"You will accept me?"

"Yes."

"Where is the distinction? I am no better than she is; I am her partner in crime, if there be a crime, and you—you who look down upon her, are a woman whose beauty was bought for so much coin by a lecherous old man who cloaked your sin and his with an impious marriage-vow."

"You insult me, sir!"

"I speak the truth."

"I came here," said Rose tremulously, " actuated by the friendliest motives, intending, if I could, to do you a service. I am received with insults and confronted with your mistress. After such a scene it is best we should see nothing more of each other," and she moved towards the door.

Leo barred the way. "Stop!" he cried, "You must hear me before you go; you have pointed out an error which I wish to rectify in your presence. Larry, dear," he continued, turning to Tiger Lily, "I have neglected my duty too long already, but it is not yet too late. Will you be my wife?"

"Leo!" exclaimed both women simultaneously, but in very different tones.

"I mean it, dear, in downright earnest."

Tiger Lily crept into Leo's arms, while a film of tears dimmed her sight, and Rose abruptly left the room.

"No, Leo," she replied, after a moment's pause, "I will not marry you."

"Why not?" he asked in surprise.

"Because—because I love you," she answered, with a sob.

"A strange reason."

"But a good one, dear," she said, drying her eyes. "I am not fit to be your wife. I am all she said I was, and since I cannot bring a spotless name to link with yours, why —we shall continue as we are, and there's an end. Now don't argue, for you can't move me."

"But——"

"Silence, dear," and she kissed his lips.

"You cannot silence me on this point."

"And you cannot alter my firm determination."

"Listen to reason, Larry," he cried petulantly.

"Don't talk nonsense, Leo," she retorted with a smile. "I only read the other day that marriage is one long quarrel."

"But our marriage will not be so."

"No, because we never will be married. We are happy now ; let well enough alone. If people talk, let them ; I don't care. For you I would bear the taunts of all the world and smile, knowing you approved, and if I do not complain, why should you ? It is against me their innuendoes are aimed."

"I know it, my girl," cried Leo, "and that is why I wish to fight them down. I feel for you even as you do for me, and since it is in my power to right you, why do you oppose me ?"

"Because it is not in your power. If you made me your wife it would only bind our names indissolubly together, but it would not blot out my past ; that past would besmirch your name while now it cannot harm you. Leo dear, I am right, I know I am ; do not let us speak of this again."

"But I am not satisfied, Larry. If you have burdens to bear why can I not share them ?"

"Because your so doing would not lighten my load, and would add, oh, so much ! to your own."

Leo sighed heavily, and leaned his head upon his hand. "You are a good woman,

Larry," he said at last. "If only Rose and the rest of her kind were like you, then——"

'Never mind my praises, Leo dear," said Tiger Lily, smilingly, "I must go and see if Ada understands about that cut in her lines."

"She understands."

"If she does, I'll return very soon."

Left alone Leo drew a chair to the table and wrote rapidly. After completing a short manuscript, he began a note to the editor of *Hermes*, requesting him to publish the parable enclosed, at once, putting aside all others for it. Before he had finished Tiger Lily returned and, seeing him at work, looked over his shoulder and read the note.

"What parable is that, Leo?" she asked. "Something new?"

Yes, one I have just written, listen," and he read aloud, with much vehemence, flushing wrathfully as he emitted his words:

"And Dante led me through those awful depths that Virgil opened to his gaze.

" And two there were we came upon ; women, who walked hand in hand ; the one shrinking from her companion with looks of loathing and disgust, which were returned with a glance of shamed appealing.

" ' Who art thou ? ' asked the poet.

" ' I,' made answer the haughty one, ' am one who lived purely and held myself far above those of my sisters who had fallen victims to the wiles of evil. Yea, I closed my doors upon them, shutting them out with revilings, as unclean, when perhaps a kindly word might have turned them back to righteousness. Ah, woe is me, I am a sinner ! '

" ' And thou ? ' asked the poet of her companion.

" ' I, alas,' she replied, ' am one of the fallen, despised, and cast forth by her, to sink to the lowest. I sinned and repented, but when she drove me forth from her door, I recked no more of right or wrong, but yielding to the first temptation, sinned again ; so my repentance availed me nothing. And she sinned as grievously as I, when she turned from my tears of penitence, but in her haughtiness she knew not of her sinning, wherefore is she even as I. Now are we both fated to walk forever, hand in hand, until our sins be atoned, she, in her pride with the courtesan, she would not lift from shame, and I with one who holds herself above me and looks down upon me with contempt.'

"And in their misery they went upon their way."

"Oh, don't publish it, Leo," said Tiger Lily.

"But I will," he replied doggedly, sealing the note, "we shall see if she is coming here to ride the high horse over you. By Heavens——" a terribly severe fit of coughing interrupted him ; his face grew purple and he clutched his side painfully, Tiger Lily was alarmed and hastened for a glass of water. She returned to find him completely exhausted, too weak to cough more, yet irritated by the inclination to do so. Gradually the spell passed and with some difficulty Tiger Lily persuaded him to lie down for a while, and soothed by her gentle ministrations, he fell asleep.

CHAPTER IV.

A MIDNIGHT SUPPER.

"Come fill the cup, and in the fire of Spring,
Your Winter-garment of repentance fling;
The Bird of Time has but a little way
To flutter—and the Bird is on the wing."
RUBAIYAT OF OMAR KHAYYAM.

AFTER the second performance of " King Robert of Sicily " (on the evening of the day that Rose called upon Leo), a merry company began to assemble, at Leo's invitation, in one of the larger private dining-rooms at Ober's. A babble of voices filled the room, and, to one first entering, it seemed as if everybody was talking and laughing at once. Leo, looking very ill and feeling miserable, although he would not admit it, greeted each comer with a kindly word of welcome, laughing away remarks about his pallor, and doing his best to play the host when he obviously should have been at home and under a doctor's care. One by one the guests arrived, until all but Tiger Lily and Ada, who were delayed at the theatre, were present.

Less rapped upon the table. "Ladies and gentlemen," he began.

"Hear, hear!" cried Durrell, applauding enthusiastically.

Less gravely bowed and continued. "We are assembled here this evening at the invitation of our honored and distinguished friend, Mr. Leo Ormsby, to—to—what for, Leo?" he asked in a very audible aside.

"To eat supper," replied Leo, gayly, "fall to, everybody, while Less is talking, and let him amuse us while we eat."

"Not much," cried Less; "if there's any talking to be done I'm quite ready to talk, but I never talk and eat at the same time, it's bad manners. To quote the Bard of

Avon—that gentleman who was the primary cause of so many of our gifted fellow men and women counting railroad ties for many, many weary miles—I would say, ' Not that I love talking less, but I love eating more ! "

" Where's your manners, Less ? " called a childish voice from the doorway as Tiger Lily and Ada entered, followed by a bedraggled little ragamuffin whose countenance had almost lost human semblance beneath the mask of dirt that covered it. " Why don't you wait for us ?"

" Pardon, O high and mighty Princess Cherub," cried Less, " Your slave was wrong, but what imp of darkness hath followed in your track ? Let me call the warders and send him to the realms below. What, Ho ! "

"Shut up, Less," said Tiger Lily, who had removed her wraps and was doing a like service for Ada, "I found the little urchin asleep in a doorway, and Ada insisted that we must bring him along to give him a bite."

"Interesting specimen," murmured Less, gazing admiringly at the urchin. "What's the species, Bogtrotter or Dirt-Eater of the Orinoco?"

"Conundrum," volunteered Durrell.

"Just take a cursory survey of it," continued Less.

"Damn it, yes," said Leo.

"It's too bad to receive my guest so," laughed Tiger Lily, "Are you hungry, little fellow?" she asked kindly.

"You bet I am," was the prompt answer.

"Give him something, Less, please," she said.

Less filled a plate from the table and carried it to a corner. The child followed him hungrily. "Now," said Less, "you shall have this plate if you'll tell me which of us will have the most hair on our heads when we're a hundred years old."

"Let him alone, Less," said Durrell.

The little street-arab looked up at Less

with an impudent wag of his head and said,
"Youse'll have de mos' cheek : Ye lets de hair
grow on yer lip ter give yer chin a chance."

Less gave him the plate and retired igno-
miniously.

"Say," said Ada to the boy, "haven't you
got a home ?"

He nodded an affirmative with his mouth
full.

"Why don't you go there, then ?"

"Like dis better."

"Strange child," murmured Less.

"Say, ask de boss kin I have some more
grub."

Ada saw that he was provided, and continued her questioning.

"Have you got a father ?"

"Yep."

"Don't he feed you ?"

"Not much. He's doin' time down duck,
fer a drunk."

"And your mother ?"

" She's out now, but she's layin low.   Dey tole her she's wanted agin, but I guess it's a bluff."

" If you got any money would you give it to her ? "

"See any green in my eye ? "

" What would you do with it ? "

"Dunno.   If I had 'bout forty cents I'd go inter business."

" What business ? "

"Papers.   Sell 'em on de street, an' if ye git stuck strike de blokes dats comin' outen de teayter wid ladies."

" A pity all that business ability should go to waste for want of a little capital," observed Less, regretfully.

" Why don't you go in with him, as silent partner, Less ? " said Leo.

" Never thought of it. If my money wasn't all tied up in railroads now——"

" If you had a business," asked Ada, " would you have to sleep in doorways ? "

"No, siree. I cud go in de newsboys' lodgin'-house. Dat's a prime place."

"Tiger Lily," said Ada, turning to her friend, "set him up, please."

"Take a hat and pass it round for him," said Tiger Lily. "Here, I'll start it," and she shook some loose-change from her pocketbook. Ada was not slow to take the hint, and a great rattling of coins accompanied her tour of the room.

"Here, little boy," she said patronizingly, as she poured her collection into his grimy hands, "now you can go into business, but you must promise me one thing."

"I'll do it," cried the little imp, his eyes fairly glowing with gratitude. "See if I don't. W'at yer want?"

"I want you to wash your face and hands," said Ada solemnly.

"But for Heaven's sake," added Less, anxiously, "do it gradually. No one can tell what danger you might run into by a too sudden exposure of the epidermis."

"And now Ada," said Tiger Lily, "let the waiter show the little fellow out and come here to the table."

"Good-night," said Ada to the departing urchin.

"Good-night," he replied, turning back in the doorway. "Say, youse is a reg'lar gang o' bricks," and he was gone.

"Here's to Leo," said Less, raising a brimming wine-glass, "with the old sentiment, 'The pen is mightier than the sword.'"

"And a woman's tongue than either," added Durrell.

"No toasts, no speeches, no formality," said Leo, "suppose you tell us a story, Less."

"Waiter, pass me some sirloin beans," said Less, trying to dodge the issue.

"But the story."

"I've got one," said Durrell.

"Fire away."

"A good many of you know little Tom Peterson, the critic of the *Star*—a little bit of a man——"

"I know," interrupted Less, "small man. Say, Durrell, did you ever notice small men are mean?'

"Oh, dry up. Peterson is a nice enough little fellow, but he takes offence too quickly, he's such a fiery tempered little chap——"

"Yes," interrupted Less again, "most even disposition possible, mad all the time."

"Look here, Less," cried Durrell, angrily, "who's telling this story?"

"We are," was the bland reply.

"Well, finish it."

"I call that cheek," exclaimed Less, with mock indignation, "ask me to finish it after I've begun so nicely for you. I'll do my share, but it's too much to ask me to do all the work."

14

" Let him alone, Less," cried Leo. "Go on Durrell."

" Well, Peterson often held forth to the boys upon the charms of a young lady of his, until we were all anxious to see her. Young Wardwell was our treasurer at the time, ' Handsome Will' we called him, and he was a perfect Adonis; the girls all raved about him, and we wanted to pit him against Peterson with the lady in question, just to have a lark with the little chap, who, by the way, had never met Will. One day Peterson asked me for seats, ' I'm going to bring *the* young lady to see your show to-night " he told me, and I wrote out a pass for him. This was just the chance we had been looking for, and Wardwell was posted up accordingly, and I fixed it so that he sat just near enough to the couple. The girl was pretty and brimful of fun, and she soon noticed that Will was regarding her steadily. She pretended not to see him at first, but every

now and then stole a glance in his direction
until a little flirtation was commenced.
Peterson took it all in, and was as mad as a
March hare. Between the acts Wardwell
came out and reported progress. Little Pete
had no idea we were putting up a job on him
and my, wasn't he savage! But the girl
rather enjoyed the fun. During the last act
he called an usher and whispered, ' Tell that
gentleman in the third row, second seat,
that Mr. Peterson of the *Star* sends his
compliments and begs to be favored with his
name.' ' That's Mr. Wardwell, Handsome
Will, sir' says the usher. ' Damn Handsome Will,' growls Pete, 'thank you, all
the same.' When the usher came out and
told his story we stood ready to prevent a
disturbance, but the boys wanted to see the
end of the fun, so when the show ended Will
was posted conspicuously in the lobby and
we stood about near him. Pretty soon Peterson comes along with his girl and sees Ward-

well. He marches right up to him, and, tipping his hat politely, says, 'Mr. Wardwell, I believe?' 'That is my name, sir.' 'Mr. Wardwell, allow me to introduce you to Miss Nelly Kendrick, Miss Kendrick this is Mr. Wardwell. I bid you both a very good evening,' and with another tip of his hat he marched away, leaving the girl behind. Will had to see her home, of course. We were playing in New York at one of the houses near Fourteenth Street and she lived way out in Harlem somewhere. The next day Will and Pete had it hot and heavy, and Will swore vengeance. When Peterson found out it was a put-up job he tried to make up with the girl, but Will wouldn't let him and, just to spite Pete, married her himself ; but the little fellow got the best of him that time, too, for she proved to have a devil of a temper and they fight like cat and dog."

"Is that the end?" asked Less, soberly.

"Yes," snapped Durrell.

"Ah, indeed? Good finish, excellent finish," said Less, applauding faintly. "Tell that last part again, will you Durrell, I didn't quite catch the point."

"I can't provide you with brains," growled Durrell, who did not relish Less's banter.

"No? why not? Has your supply given out?"

"I'll engage you as a clown if you display so much talent for it," said Durrell.

"Why didn't you speak sooner? I've about decided to take an interest in the paper business with Ada's friend."

"What makes you so quiet, Leo?" asked Ada. "You're letting Less do all the talking."

"He's qualified to, Cherub, isn't he?"

"I s'pose so, but I don't like to see you so quiet."

"Come, sit beside me then, little one, and see if you can 'liven me up to talking point." A heavy cough ended his speech. Ada moved to his side, chattering gayly, while he listened absently, stroking the child's curls.

" I don't know what to do for Leo, Less," whispered Tiger Lily, ' that dreadful cough hangs on to him so, and he positively refuses to see a doctor or take care of himself at all. He had a terrible spell this afternoon, and I tried to keep him home to-night, but you know I can do nothing with him. Don't you think he is looking badly ? "

" He told me to-day that he was going to take a good long rest as soon as you and Ada could get away."

" That will be soon. ' King Robert' is to be withdrawn in order to make some further alterations, and Durrell can do without me for the rest of the season."

" Come, Less," cried Leo, " give us that story."

" Don't know one," was the prompt reply," " but talk about larks, you ought to have been with me this afternoon. You know that

more people pass the corner of Winter
and Washington Streets than any other
spot in the city. Well, having nothing
to do, I thought I would make the passers
amuse me, so I bought a ball of stout twine
and tied an end of it to a sign on the corner,
about three feet above the ground, and then,
let the ball roll gently across the sidewalk.
A gentleman walking up Washington Street
caught it on his foot and carried it up as
far as Ditson's. He untangled himself easily,
but meanwhile several other people were
snared, and the ball was unrolling itself
further all the time. A man was caught
about the waist, he lifted the string over his
head and caught a lady's bonnet. He apol-
ogized and tried to extricate her ; when he
succeeded he was hopelessly entangled again
himself with a knot of other people. The
more they struggled to free themselves the
worse the snarl grew, and every moment
some one else was caught. An important

policeman came along and undertook to set matters straight, but only succeeded in adding himself to my batch of victims. I thought I had seen almost enough of the fun, which promised to last for some time, and started up Winter Street; but I had taken only a few steps when a tug at my ankle told me I too, was enmeshed. I stooped to free my foot, and the passers walked the string over me in half a dozen loops, and if I had not promptly whipped out my penknife and cut the string, I might have been struggling there yet."

"Ah!" exclaimed Durrell blandly, in imitation of Less's patronizing manner of a few moments before "good finish, excellent finish, excellent finish, my boy."

"There now," exclaimed Less, appealing to the company, "Durrell indorses my story-telling but he won't indorse my notes. Funny fellow, Durrell. By the way, Leo, talking of notes, I received one to-night, re-

lating to you. I can't make anything out of
it, perhaps you may be able to, here it is,"
and he handed the epistle to Leo.

"From a lady, I'll wager," cried Durrell.

Leo smiled and unfolded the paper. As
he glanced at it he grew red and then pale,
frowning, as if displeased. The note read:—

" MR. INGRAHAM,
        " Dear Sir :—
                " Will you pardon my addressing
you and permit me to beg a great favor. I shall feel deeply
grateful if you will inform your friend, Mr. Leo Ormsby,
from me, that I beg of him to grant me an interview, if only
for a moment, before he is married. Please, please do not
fail to give him the message, and I will remain
                        Ever your debtor,
                                " ROSE CHOATE."

Leo refolded the note and returned it to
Less. " Bah ! " he said with a look of annoy-
ance, " I shall not notice it." He raised his
glass to his lips, but hardly tasted the wine.
As he replaced the glass upon the table he
began coughing violently. Controlling him-

self with an effort he rose, saying, "Excuse me for a moment, please, the room is so oppressively warm that it irritates my cough, I must have a little fresh air."

"Shall I go with you, old man?" asked Less, rising.

Leo made an emphatic negative gesture and left the room. They could hear him coughing as he passed along the corridor without, and the sound dampened their hilarity for the moment, but Less would not let the gayety flag. He was as concerned as any for his friend, but he knew Leo had invited the company with the intention of giving them a pleasant party, and that he could best please him by pleasing his guests. Tiger Lily anxiously watched the door for Leo's return, and Ada, reading the concern in her face, crept to her side and watched with her. The host's absence was becoming noticeably protracted, and Tiger Lily was growing really alarmed, when Less saw through the door, which stood slightly ajar, a waiter, who beckoned him. Fearful that something was wrong with his friend, but anxious not to disturb the company, he rose with a forced laugh, saying :

"I'm going to fetch our truant back if I am excused."

"Go on, Less," said Tiger Lily, "it's time he returned."

He left the room, to remdin away an unreasonably long time. Without him the conversation flagged, a dull silence, broken now and then by a monosyllabic remark or a whisper, hung over the party. The minutes dragged interminably, until Tiger Lily rose, saying, "I can't stand this, I fear something is wrong, and I'm going to see. Will you come with me, Durrell ?"

"Yes," replied he, rising promptly, but looking up he saw Less standing in the doorway with a very serious look upon his usually merry face.

"Well ?" he said.

"Leo was taken sick, and we have sent him home. He begs you will not disturb yourselves, but continue as if he were here."

"Waiter," called Tiger Lily sharply, "call a carriage, please." Then to the company, "I'm going home to him. Come, Ada. What was it, Less?"

"His old trouble, the cough," answered Less, evasively.

"Good-night," said Tiger Lily, abruptly, as she hurried out with Ada.

"Good-night."

"Anything serious, Less?" whispered Durrell anxiously.

"Yes. A terrible hemorrhage. Two doctors have gone home with him, and—it looks bad."

"Not—not——"

"I don't know. I'm going to him as soon as I can, but he wished me to do the honors here. I couldn't say no, and—here I am when I ought to be with him."

" What can you do for him ? "

" Mighty little, mighty little ; but I'd like to be there to do that. Durrell, he—he's my best, my dearest friend."

"Go then, Less, I'll take charge here."

"Thanks, old man, that's kind and——"

Less turned a pair of eyes in which there were traces of a threatened overflow upon his friend, and wrung his hand vigorously, then muttering a " good-night " that sounded like a sob, he hurriedly left the room.

CHAPTER V.

EXIT.

"The moving Finger writes ; and having writ,
Moves on ; nor all your Piety nor Wit
Shall lure it back to cancel half a Line,
Nor all your Tears wash out a Word of it."

RUBAYAT OF OMAR KHAYYAM.

AT about noon on the following day, Durrell rang the bell at Mrs. West's.

As the servant opened the door he caught sight of Less, still in evening-dress, from the night before, and called to him.

"You have not slept !" exclaimed Durrell, noticing his friend's pallor and disordered dress, at a glance.

"None of us have," wearily replied Less.

"Well, what news ; how is he ?"

"Beyond all pain."

" Good God, not dead ? "

Less nodded an affirmative. He was too`
much affected to command his voice for the
moment.

" Is it possible ? " exclaimed Durrell, aghast.
For a moment the two men stood silent, as if
stunned by the sudden blow. Durrell broke
the silence, saying in a subdued tone : "Tell
me about it."

"Sit down," replied Less sadly, "and I
will. The doctors worked over him when he
reached home and seemed to ease him. He
was terribly weak, though, and after a while
fell asleep. I sat there with one of the phy-
sicians, watching ; watching and thinking.
I could not read, the lights were too dim ; we
could not talk, it might waken Leo ; and I
dared not sleep for fear he might want me.
For hours we sat there in silence, the doctor
and I, with nothing to occupy our minds.
I counted the ticks of the clock for a while ;
but gave that up as a bad job. I tried not

s

to think of poor Leo, but the thought would come. The doctors gave us very little hope, and the fear that he was already dying constantly haunted me. I would have given everything to be able to act, but against the awful uncertainty of death what was I to do? You know my religious views—that is, you know I have none, and yet I prayed then ; prayed fervently, honestly, for Leo's life. There are limits beyond which we stumble against the dark barrier of the unknown and unknowable. Oh, what a comfort it would be, did we but know that sundered ones would be reunited at 'that bourn from which no traveller returns,' but, alas ! no one can say truly that he knows. Many, like me, scoff at religion, but the visit of death to a dear one brings us to our knees. Death is religion's strongest ally." Less sighed heavily and paused a moment. "Well," he resumed, "finally Leo woke, and the doctor gave him some medicine. He seemed remarkably bright, and I was surprised and delighted to note his improvement. He asked me to bring the manuscript of his new play, 'The Diver,' and read him the last lines he had written, and I obeyed. 'Now write,' he said, and I took up the pen--the doctor approached the bedside—'Exit,' and as I wrote the word I heard the doctor exclaim, and, looking up, saw at a glance that the end had come. That was the last word poor Leo ever spoke. In half an hour he was gone."

"Exit," murmured Durrell sadly.

"He died peacefully," said Less, making no effort to conceal the evidences of his grief, "just fell asleep. He looks as if he were sleeping ; would you like to see him ?"

"Yes."

"Come," and he rose to show the way.

"But——"

"Well, what is it ?"

"Perhaps Tiger Lily——"

"No, poor girl, I think she has gone to her room."

"Come then."

In a small anteroom, through which the two men passed to reach the room where the body lay, they saw Tiger Lily sitting at a table, her head buried in her folded arms, sobbing wildly, in a perfect abandonment of grief. They tip-toed by her, almost unnoticed, and entered the chamber of death.

Tiger Lily was roused by the voice of one of the servants raised in loud expostulation. She lifted her dishevelled head and gazed about, with eyes red and bloodshot from weeping, seeking the cause of the disturbance.

"You mustn't go in there, Miss," the maid was saying ; "indeed you can't."

"I must and shall. Stand aside ! "

"Who is there ? " called Tiger Lily, wearily. The door opened and Rose Choate entered. Tiger Lily rose to her feet with the look of a fury, and the servant made off after one frightened look at her.

" You ? "

" Oh, is he really dead ? " There were tears in her voice and eyes as she spoke.

" Dead! yes, and you killed him! " cried Tiger Lily vehemently ; " You, who might have had his love even to this day, if you chose ; might have had him by your side now, full of life, of love, of happiness ! But you sent him from you, out into the storm, and now he is there, cold, gray, dead, dead, and you killed him. Oh, Leo, Leo ! " A passionate burst of sobs choked her utterance.

" I killed him ! " cried Rose in tearful indignation. " Did I lead him into the fast company he has been keeping of late ? Did I take him with me to late suppers, teach him to use wine as water, make him lead a life of which each moment must bring some new excitement, and which treacherously and

surely undermined his health ?   That is
what killed him, and you, not I, are the
cause."

Tiger Lily shook her head sadly, "I loved
him," she said simply, "I love him now and
always."

"And I loved him," wailed Rose, "I
never ceased to love him.   I came here
yesterday, prepared to humble myself, to
win him back ; I came to-day determined to
do so.   Every fibre of my heart has yearned
for him since we parted, and now—now he
is dead !   Oh, why did you ever come
between us ?   You are my evil genius."

"And you were his."

"You did not care for him as I do,"
sobbed Rose.   "In a short while you will
forget him for some new lover, but I——"

"Oh, you——" began Tiger Lily fiercely,
and then feebly finished by covering her face
with her hands.

The door was heard to close, and Less

stood between them. He caught Tiger Lily's words, and saw at a glance how matters stood.

"Ladies," he said gently, "is this a time or place to quarrel? Let the dead rest in peace, he was a friend to both of you, can you not remember this, and——"

"Don't, Less," said Tiger Lily, tearfully, "I ought not to have allowed her to so aggravate me."

"Mrs. Choate," he said, turning to Rose, "do you think it right to intrude here?"

"I came to see Leo, I find him dead," she wailed.

"Alas! and finding him so?"

"I shall remain," was the dogged re sponse.

"For what?"

"I do not know," she sobbed, "to be near him."

"Think of the talk your action will cause among your friends."

"I do not care," she returned, in the same dogged way.

"You must care. We are 'Bohemians' here, and do as we please. In 'Bohemia' they do not delight in destroying reputations; but you come from a different sphere, where you must beware of your 'friends.' You look down upon poor Tiger Lily, and speak slightingly, scornfully, of her. If you remain, even as you do to her, so will your friends do to you."

"What shall I live for now?" moaned Rose.

"That will appear later. We all feel his loss as keenly as you do, but we must think of the living. Your duty is to yourself now, and it bids you go."

"I cannot, oh, I cannot," cried Rose despairingly, "oh, you can't know how bitter has been my self-reproach, how I loved him, how I lived only in the hope of a reconciliation when the time should come. I knew I must

wait and I did wait, so patiently, and all the
time my love grew stronger, deeper, until
at last it filled my whole being. Then I
found myself free, and I came to him, only
to learn that she had risen up between us, and
now—now——" she covered her face with
her hands, weeping bitterly.

"Tiger Lily loved Leo, too," said Less
gently, "even as you loved him, and the
same sorrow that has fallen upon you
weighs her down ; your sufferings are hers.
If you two could only share your sorrow and
sympathize with each other, how much
better it would be than exchanging bitter
taunts and reproaches as you have been
doing. The cause of your enmity is gone
with Leo's life. The cause of your sorrow
remains, lying in there, a poor morsel of
clay. Will you quarrel over all that is left
us of our friend, or will you rather mingle
your tears in peace, perhaps friendship ? "

Tiger Lily dried her eyes and answered :

"Friends we cannot be, there is much to prevent, even if we were both willing. She holds aloof from me, and she does right; my friendship would degrade her in the circle she moves in, no matter how disinterested it might be, but we need not be enemies. Sorrow has come to us, we can bear it together, and when—when all is over, she will go her way, I will go mine, and we shall meet no more.

"You are very good," said Rose tremulously, turning to Tiger Lily, " but I—I may as well die now," she added hysterically.

"Once he said something like that to me," said Tiger Lily softly, "and then he added, 'I did more than die, I lived,' and his words have always remained fixed in my memory. I feel as you do, but I shall do as he did. He loved little Ada, and the child's future shall be my care. I know the perils of an actress's life, and I will shield her until she is a noble, pure woman, and I can say :

'This is what he would have wished for her.'"

"Let me aid you," cried Rose, eagerly.

"We shall see later," she replied. "I am glad," she thought, with a compassionate look at Rose, "that I have that last parable of Leo's, and can suppress it, for her sake, poor thing." She held forth her hand, and Rose took it in both of hers, sobbing.

"Come," said Tiger Lily, "let us go to him." And with great calmness she led Rose to the door of Leo's chamber.

Less was there before them, and as he held the door open, he beckoned Durrell to leave the two women alone with the dead.

THE END.

 **BOOKS**

From the Press of the Arena Publishing Company.

Along Shore with a Man of War.

By MARGUERITE DICKINS. A delightful story of travel, delightfully told, handsomely illustrated, and beautifully bound. Price, postpaid, $1.50.

Evolution.

Popular lectures by leading thinkers, delivered before the Brooklyn Ethical Association. This work is of inestimable value to the general reader who is interested in Evolution as applied to religious, scientific, and social themes. It is the joint work of a number of the foremost thinkers in America to-day. One volume, handsome cloth, illustrated, complete index. 408 pp. Price, postpaid, $2.00.

Sociology.

Popular lectures by eminent thinkers, delivered before the Brooklyn Ethical Association. This work is a companion volume to "Evolution," and presents the best thought of representative thinkers on social evolution. One volume, handsome cloth, with diagram and complete index. 412 pp. Price, postpaid, $2.00.

For sale by all booksellers. Sent postpaid upon receipt of the price.

Arena Publishing Company,

Copley Square,　　　　　　　　　　　BOSTON, MASS.

From the Press of the Arena Publishing Company.

is This Your Son, My Lord?

By HELEN H. GARDENER. The most powerful novel written by an American. A terrible *expose* of conventional immorality and hypocrisy. Price: paper, 50 cents; cloth, $1.00.

Pray You, Sir, Whose Daughter?

By HELEN H. GARDENER. A brilliant novel of to-day, dealing with social purity and the "age of consent" laws. Price: paper, 50 cents; cloth, $1.00.

A Spoil of Office.

A novel. By HAMLIN GARLAND. The truest picture of Western life that has appeared in American fiction. Price: paper, 50 cents; cloth, $1.00.

Lessons Learned from Other Lives.

By B. O. FLOWER.

There are fourteen biographies in this volume, dealing with the lives of Seneca and Epictetus, the great Roman philosophers; Joan of Arc, the warrior maid; Henry Clay, the statesman; Edwin Booth and Joseph Jefferson, the actors; John Howard Payne, William Cullen Bryant, Edgar Allan Poe, Alice and Phœbe Cary, and John G. Whittier, the poets; Alfred Russell Wallace, the scientist; Victor Hugo, the many-sided man of genius.

"The book sparkles witn literary jewels." — *Christian Leader*, Cincinnati, Ohio.

Price: paper, 50 cents; cloth. $1.00.

For sale by all booksellers. Sent postpaid upon receipt 3f the price.

Arena Publishing Company,

Copley Square,   BOSTON, MASS.

From the Press of the Arena Publishing Company.

Songs.

By NEITH BOYCE. Illustrated with original drawings by ETHELWYN WELLS CONREY. A beautiful gift book. Bound in white and gold. Price, postpaid, $1.25.

The Finished Creation, and Other Poems.

By BENJAMIN HATHAWAY, author of "The League of the Iroquois," "Art Life," and other Poems. Handsomely bound in white parchment vellum, stamped in silver. Price, postpaid, $1.25.

Wit and Humor of the Bible.

By Rev. MARION D. SHUTTER, D.D. A brilliant and reverent treatise. Published only in cloth. Price, postpaid, $1.50.

Son of Man; or, Sequel to Evolution.

By CELESTIA ROOT LANG. Published only in cloth.

This work, in many respects, very remarkably discusses the next step in the Evolution of Man. It is in perfect touch with advanced Christian Evolutionary thought, but takes a step beyond the present position of Religion Leaders.

Price, postpaid, $1.25.

For sale by all booksellers. Sent postpaid upon receipt of the price.

Arena Publishing Company,

Copley Square,   BOSTON, MASS.

From the Press of the Arena Publishing Company.

Salome Shepard, Reformer.

By HELEN M. WINSLOW. A New England story. Price: paper, 50 cents; cloth, $1.00.

The Law of Laws.

By S. B. WAIT. The author takes advance metaphysical grounds on the origin, nature, and destiny of the soul.

> "It is offered as a contribution to the thought of that unnumbered fraternity of spirit whose members are found wherever souls are sensitive to the impact of the truth and feel another's burden as their own."—*Author's Preface.*

256 pages; handsome cloth. Price, postpaid, $1.50.

Life. A Novel.

By WILLIAM W. WHEELER. A book of thrilling interest from cover to cover.

> In the form of a novel called "LIFE," William W. Wheeler has put before the public some of the clearest statements of logical ideas regarding humanity's present aspects, its inherent and manifest powers, and its future, that we have ever read. The book is strong, keen, powerful; running over with thought, so expressed as to clearly convey the author's ideas; everything is to the point, nothing superfluous—and for this it is specially admirable.—*The Boston Times.*

Price: paper, 50 cents; cloth, $1.00.

For sale by all booksellers. Sent postpaid upon receipt of the price.

Arena Publishing Company,

Copley Square,   BOSTON, MASS.